Crazy Dead

A Cordi O'Callaghan Mystery

Crazy
DEAD

Suzanne F. Kingsmill

DUNDURN
TORONTO

Project editor: Kathryn Lane
Copy editor: Maryan Gibson
Design: Courtney Horner
Cover design: Laura Boyle
Cover image: © iStock/Getty/iStock
Printer: Webcom

Library and Archives Canada Cataloguing in Publication

Kingsmill, Suzanne, author
        Crazy dead / Suzanne F. Kingsmill.

(A Cordi O'Callaghan mystery)
Issued in print and electronic formats.
ISBN 978-1-4597-3552-1 (paperback).--ISBN 978-1-4597-3553-8 (pdf).--
ISBN 978-1-4597-3554-5 (epub)

        I. Title. II. Series: Kingsmill, Suzanne. Cordi O'Callaghan mystery.

PS8621.I57C73 2016   C813'.6   C2015-908158-0
                                                     C2015-908159-9

1   2   3   4   5   20   19   18   17   16

 Conseil des Arts
du Canada Canada Council
for the Arts Canada   ONTARIO ARTS COUNCIL
CONSEIL DES ARTS DE L'ONTARIO
an Ontario government agency
un organisme du gouvernement de l'Ontario

We acknowledge the support of the Canada Council for the Arts and the Ontario Arts Council for our publishing program. We also acknowledge the financial support of the Government of Canada through the Canada Book Fund and Livres Canada Books, and the Government of Ontario through the Ontario Book Publishing Tax Credit and the Ontario Media Development Corporation.

Care has been taken to trace the ownership of copyright material used in this book. The author and the publisher welcome any information enabling them to rectify any references or credits in subsequent editions.

— J. Kirk Howard, President

The publisher is not responsible for websites or their content unless they are owned by the publisher.

Printed and bound in Canada.

Visit us at
Dundurn.com | @dundurnpress | Facebook.com/dundurnpress | Pinterest.com/dundurnpress

Dundurn
3 Church Street, Suite 500
Toronto, Ontario, Canada
M5E 1M2

For Dorion
Sisters forever!

chapter one

The pain of the dark. Eternal blackness smothering my mind. I felt so alone, lying there, staring at the ceiling. It hadn't changed through all my days of darkness, and neither had I. We were both water-stained. Me by tears, and the ceiling by the rain seeping in through some wayward hole. But at least the stain on the ceiling vaguely represented something: a seagull sailing on the wind, its wings tilted up toward the sky in the exact opposite direction that I represented, which was nothing, miles and miles of nothing, in a spiralling descent downward.

I could hear the clatter of dishes down the hall, but the dissonant sounds didn't mean anything to me. It was just noise. Dark noise. And into that wrenching blackness came a voice — my brother Ryan's — but it could not reach me where I was.

"It's time to go, Cordi."

I didn't care about going or staying. I was beyond that. Ryan had to pull me off my rumpled bed and lead me out into the sticky black sunshine. I found myself in his dusty old car and wondered vaguely why I was there. I sat immobile and watched the cars go by as we drove through the congested streets of Toronto, until the motion of the car put me to sleep.

Ryan woke me and helped me out of the car into a parking lot covered with a monotony of cars. We weaved our way through them. We went inside a big concrete building that loomed eight or ten storeys above us, and Ryan sat me down in a crowded hallway and left me there. One among many, sitting on hard metal chairs, waiting. Waiting for what?

It was some sort of hospital because there were people in white lab coats. But I stayed there, where Ryan had left me. I guess time passed and he came back for me, bringing with him a red-headed woman dressed all in white, who extended her hand to me. I stared at it, but I did not take it. Seemed so pointless. Why take a hand when the emptiness inside me would render the gesture meaningless?

"I have to go now, Cordi," said Ryan, and I looked up at him and saw nothing, felt nothing. He kissed me on the forehead and turned to go. I did not turn to watch him leave.

The nurse babbled on about nothing in particular as she led me to an elevator and we went up and up, the little red floor numbers above the door flashing as we passed them, until the elevator spewed us out into a small lobby. There were glass doors at either end and a glassed-in nursing station straight ahead. She opened one of the doors and led me down a wide grey-tiled hall with painted cinderblock walls. The room I followed her into was a box with beds. I was vaguely aware that there seemed to be a lot of them, and that made me think for some reason of an orphanage, although I had never been to one.

I was an orphan, too. I was an orphan from life.

She must have told me her name, the nurse, but I hadn't taken it in as she gently placed my belongings on one of the beds and said something else I didn't take in. Didn't care to take in. I looked at my belongings. They looked so pathetic and lonely, just like me. The nurse left and I curled up on the bed, cradling my head on my hands. There wasn't even a curtain to give me some privacy

"You try to kill yourself?" The voice was soft and quiet. She moved her head into my line of sight. Jet-black hair cut in a Cleopatra hairstyle that made her improbably round face look like a balloon. But there was nothing balloonish about her troubled eyes. They were so sunken that they almost imploded into themselves, reflecting a world surely alien to mine. Or maybe not. We stared at each other, but I did not move from where I lay. Not a muscle.

"Naw. You're too out of it to have tried that," she said, answering her own question. She'd been there, to that place where you couldn't even lift a finger to help yourself, the place where I was now. I knew it without her having to tell me.

She sat there and talked at me. She kept talking about her "sieve of a mind." I do remember she told me a joke that made her cackle with a laugh that went on and on and on. And made me want to cry and cry. It was about two little birds on a telephone wire and one little bird says to the other little bird, "Don't some people's voices make your feet tingle?"

I didn't laugh. I remember that. Looking back now, I wonder if she had sensed what was coming, in some way.

When she left I slept for centuries, dreaming dark dreams and empty hopes. I was in a huge barn, with a man, a man who was not my father, and I was swinging on a swing strung high from the rafters and I saw my parents and my brother crying, because they could not find me. Back when I was a little girl. Back when I was going to be a writer. So long ago. So far away.

And the nightmares mercifully faded and I was conscious only of eating, of swallowing pills, aware of people crowded around my bed asking endless questions to my stony silence.

No, I did not try to kill myself. Of that I was sure.

I lived in a daze, the memories of my mind interlaced with the tendrils of a fog that watered down everything I did, everything I was, till I felt I was but a blur on my mind's horizon, wearing a caution sign that read SEVERELY REDUCED VISIBILITY FOREVER AHEAD.

And then one morning I woke up and the sun didn't look quite so black and I felt a tiny quickening in my mind that I had despaired of ever feeling again. I nursed that little glimmer the way one would a small ember in a hearth and day by day it got bigger until one day I spoke. It wasn't much, but it was a way back.

There was, finally, a grey, dingy light at the end of the tunnel.

chapter two

M y mind was bruised and worn, but still there, still me, still Cordi. I was actually able to look around at my surroundings and take stock. I'd never been in a psychiatric hospital before, but depression, the dark all-consuming kind, had periodically hounded me almost all my life. Pathetically, I remember thinking it would go away once I turned thirteen, once I got my period, once I got my driver's licence, once I had a boyfriend. But it never did. Instead, I lived my life around it, always wary that it could blindside me with the force of a seismic shift.

It somehow seemed a logical extension of my life, to be here, far from home. Ryan had rescued me from my log cabin on our Gatineau, Quebec, dairy farm, found a condo for me, and insisted I come to Toronto to do my sabbatical, but I knew now that it was so he could keep an eye on me and my injured mind. Not that he needed the additional burden. He had temporarily moved to Toronto to try to save his daughter, Annie, from an aggressive brain tumour. There were doctors in Ottawa who could have helped, but Ryan wanted the best, and the best happened to be in Toronto. There is no doubt he would have gone to Vancouver or Beijing if that was what it took. But it made me feel awful. At first I had persuaded myself that I had come to Toronto so that I could support Ryan and Rose, Annie and little Davey, but then the darkness had come in spades, and I got lost.

My hospital "room" was as warm and fuzzy as a concrete slab. Someone had tried to make it look nice by taping up a poster of bicycle wheels and a tall lanky black man playing the saxophone. But the posters were ripped and the tape holding them to the walls had yellowed with age. How many souls had come through this room and looked at those posters and despaired — like me?

There was an oversize single window, no curtain, facing north, that let in a lot of light. I needed that after all the darkness in my life. The four beds were lined up on either side of the window. Even with the bedside table blocking me from the bed across the way, there was no privacy and no warmth. Totally utilitarian, and a setup that made it easier for any nurse or doctor or caretaker walking by to keep an eye on us, but it made me very uncomfortable. There were some flowers on my table — big garish purple things. There was a card tucked into one of the gargantuan petals and I got out of bed and pulled it out, angry that someone other than my brother knew I was here.

"Get better, Cordi. We're rooting for you. Love, Martha and Duncan."

Martha was my lab technician. She looked after all the animals in my lab at Sussex University, where I worked as a zoology professor. Duncan was a pathologist and, along with Martha, had helped me solve a number of mysterious deaths that had turned out to be murders. What can I say? I often seem to be in the wrong place at the wrong time. I softened at the sight of her name. If anyone needed to know how I was doing and where I was doing it, it was Martha.

I put down the card and looked around the room. The bed on the other side of the window was occupied by someone curled up in a tight ball of bedcovers and pillow, and I could not see her face. The woman in the third bed had her face turned into the wall. Obviously I wasn't the only goldfish wanting some privacy. The fourth bed was empty, the sheets rucked up so that the fitted sheet was off its moorings. I sat down on my bed and looked out the window, then started when I felt a presence beside me. I looked around and saw the girl who had told me the joke about the little birds. I'm not sure why I remembered that, or her, because there was very little else that I could remember since Ryan had brought me here. I didn't even know how long ago that had been.

Her hair starkly framed her round face and this time I saw how wide apart her eyes were — you could've put a bowling alley there. And she could've been the bowling ball. Because now I noticed how short and round and dumpy and young she was. Her dark, almost black eyes stared out at me from above a button of a nose, and her mouth was almost round, as if she had a nervous tic that made her constantly pucker up. Purple-and-yellow running shoes peeked out from under black-and-white flannel pajamas made into a giant crossword puzzle. I wondered if it was a working puzzle or just fake. I had a sudden strong urge to write a word, even without knowing the clue. *"Trapped" might work*, I thought.

She sat down beside me with proprietorial panache and said, "You're better now." And she giggled, just like a four-year-old, although she must have been more like twenty-four.

I recoiled, still not wanting to talk very much, as if my words would somehow send me back into the darkness.

"You have pretty eyes." She swivelled and trampled some more on my personal space as she reached out to touch my eyes. Instinctively I pulled back. She scrunched up her face, as if she was about to cry.

"You don't like me," she said and then she did begin to cry.

"Yes, I do," I said, my voice alien in my ears, hoarse and unused. I hesitated, searching for something to say. "I liked your joke."

She sniffled and stared at me. "What joke?"

"The two little birds on a telephone wire."

She looked at me blankly and then I saw confusion and fear, which shook me, because why would a joke make her so afraid?

She stood up and started backing away from me, without taking her eyes off me.

"They're stealing me," she said. Then she said it again. And again.

She turned and ran to her own bed and buried her face in her pillow. I almost got up and went over, but something held me back. Something in my own mind or something from hers? I wasn't sure. My own mind was still pretty wobbly. Looking at her now, I had a vague recollection of her bringing me some water, which I had spilled all over my shirt and couldn't have given a damn. And her name was Mavis. I was suddenly sure of that, though why that piece of information should bubble up was a mystery.

As I sat there on my bed she suddenly jumped off her bed, grabbed a sweater from the closet, and charged out the door, just as a woman dressed in nurse's whites walked in.

"Oh, how wonderful, Cordi. They've moved you back," she said. She was maybe thirty-eight, with shiny auburn hair. It was corralled into a painful-looking ponytail, revealing strong angular features that made her look more handsome than pretty. She was about five foot eleven and maybe 180 pounds. For all the extra weight, she was strangely sensual, like a woman who has just made love and is coveting the feeling of her own sexuality. She had a voluptuous Botticellian figure and she carried herself like Aphrodite. Some women just have it, no matter what they look like, and she had it in earnest.

Her name tag said Ella, but I'd never seen her before in my life. Or had I? How much of my life had I lost to the darkness and despair of depression?

"What's the date?" I asked rather brusquely, trying to hide my fear.

"February 23."

February 23. *Jesus.* I vaguely remembered doing a guest lecture at the Ramsey Wright Zoology Building at the University of Toronto at the beginning of February. Teaching a class of undergrads about the mechanics of bird flight. But all I had really wanted was to be away from the world, away from prying eyes. And I had crept home. Three weeks ago. *Jesus*. Three lost weeks. I had to get out of this place. I didn't belong here. Or did I? I remembered the blackness, now receding. Had the hospital done that? Made the blackness go away?

Ella had gone to the window and was talking about how nice the view was and that if I tried really hard I could see Robarts Library at the University of Toronto. I knew what she was doing, of course. She was trying to make me feel at home in my goldfish bowl.

"We'll get you to some group therapy sessions and you'll see your doctor later today," she said. She moved away from the window and toward me, where I sat on my bed. She reached out and handed me a little paper cup. I took it from her as she said, "Here are your pills."

Inside were three pills, three different kinds. For all I knew they were arsenic, strychnine, and cyanide, but that was ridiculous and I knew it. She waited for me to pop them in my mouth and when I didn't she said, "We have to have our pills, dear. Just pop them in and I'll be on my way. And next time you can get them yourself. Eight o'clock mornings and nine o'clock evenings just down the hall. Mavis will show you where."

I dumped the pills into my hand and hesitated again, not because I didn't want to take them, but because a perfect stranger had called me "dear" and was including herself in the taking of my pills, and I was trying to digest that disturbing fact.

"They're the same pills as usual, dear. You can ask your doctor about them if you want, but right now you need to take them."

I felt a twinge of anger, but it wasn't strong enough to resist, just a watery feeling amidst the unfocused thoughts of my mind. I popped the pills.

I was rummaging around for some clothes to wear when Mavis stomped back into the room, dived under her sheets, such as they were, and lay still, like a fawn being warned by its mother. I was looking at the lump that was Mavis when one of the other lumps suddenly exploded out of her bed in a long lithe motion of sheer athleticism. She must have been nearly six-two, with shoulder-length thick blonde hair sprawling all over her face, and a thin body that was all muscle and clothed in loose maroon shorts and a matching pajama top. I watched her in fascination, her toned body moving like a waltz, each movement flowing effortlessly into the next, almost as if she was moving in slow motion, though she most definitely was not. Her beautiful body was eclipsed by her face. She had smooth milky-white-and-rose skin and enormous sapphire eyes, bookending a perfectly shaped little nose with a curvy tip. Her lips were full and naturally reddish. She caught me staring at her and frowned.

"Lucy," she said as if it was a command to arms, her voice surprisingly deep.

"Cordi," I answered.

She cocked her head. "What the hell's that short for?" She sounded aggrieved, as if I had metaphorically stomped on her toe.

I hesitated, not wanting to answer, but she was looking at me so intensely that a question I usually deflect, I answered.

"Cordelia." After thirty-five years of living with that name I still hated it. Why my parents had picked it I never knew, although I always suspected it represented some clandestine place where they had first met. As soon as I was old enough, and had endured enough taunts, I insisted on being called Cordi. Lucy looked at me as if she had just smelled a bad smell.

"Whoa. Not sure whose name is worse," she said as she glanced in Mavis's direction. "Mavis? Cordelia? At least you have a good short form. Avis sounds like the car rental."

She grabbed her sheets and made an attempt at making her bed when Mavis suddenly flipped back her covers and stared at us, then got out of bed.

"Kit's going to get in trouble," said Mavis. Lucy and I glanced over at the last lump left in bed.

"Not supposed to miss breakfast," said Lucy in a critical voice.

Mavis shrugged. "Not on my conscience," she said. She rolled her eyes and grabbed a towel and left the room.

And that was when Lucy added, "Poor Mavis." When I didn't react she asked, "Don't you want to know why?"

"Sure. Why?"

"She has an ECT this morning." Lucy's voice suddenly sounded tight and tinny and disturbingly ominous.

I involuntarily shuddered. Electroconvulsive or electroshock therapy. ECT. An electrical assault on the brain, producing controlled seizures. I didn't know much about it, just that it scared me.

We were interrupted by Ella gliding back into the room. Now that I had a chance to study her without her inquisitive eyes on me, I saw that her left hand, which was holding out a little paper cup, was missing its ring finger. I had visions of her chopping off her finger with a butcher's cleaver or getting it caught in a table saw. This time the cup was not for me.

"Where's Mavis?" Ella asked. Lucy and I said nothing, probably thinking the other one would answer. When we didn't, Ella turned to leave, just as Mavis came back into the room. My mind was still on Ella and her lost finger when Mavis's voice cut all further thoughts from my mind.

"What's this?" she said in a soft suspicious voice.

"It's ECT day, Mavis," Ella replied. "You know that. Doctor's orders."

"Pills, pills, pills," Mavis said in a singsong voice. She stared uncertainly at Ella and Ella stared back, her prominent chin at an impervious angle. She'd obviously been here many times before, waiting for balking patients to swig their meds before procedures. She held out the little cup.

"Doctor's orders," she said again, but this time more sternly and with a touch of impatience. "Just a tranquilizer to make you calm."

Mavis suddenly snatched it out of Ella's hand, threw back her head, and jettisoned the pill into her mouth. It was suddenly very quiet. Ella glanced at me and then slowly turned, and walked out of the room.

I was still sitting on my bed trying to figure out what I should do next, when Mavis jumpstarted things for me.

"KIT, IT'S TIME TO GET UP, OR YOU'LL BE IN TROUBLE!" she yelled. I picked my heart up off the floor where it had landed after Mavis's outburst and looked in the direction of poor Kit, whose eardrums had been closer to the source than mine.

Kit groaned in that universal thumbs-down to getting up, then slowly rolled out of her cocoon of sheet and blanket — we didn't get anything more than that, just a sheet and a thin blanket. Like a chrysalis emerging into the light, Kit was an amazing sight. Her flaming red hair curled and *sproinged* at least six inches from her head. And her eyes were cobalt blue, in a wonderfully startling contrast to her hair. And they lit on me like a homing pigeon. She didn't say anything as she got out of bed. She was wearing pink pajamas that clashed with her hair and left her figure looking amorphous. But even in the unflattering cloak of those pajamas I could tell that she was tiny, because the pajamas dwarfed her. She was well under five feet and her unruly hair framed a face with doll-like features. She was striking.

She hadn't taken her eyes off me.

"Who are you?" she finally asked.

"Cordi," I said.

She turned her back on us and pulled the sheet and blanket up over the pillow, then spent an inordinate amount of time smoothing out every crease and every dent until the bed was perfect. Next she straightened the already straightened objects on her bedside table and finally turned and walked over to Mavis's messy bed, a look of intense concentration on her face, and not a little bit of anxiety.

Mavis made a sound like a squawking bell and said in a stern siren voice, "Out of bounds, out of bounds," as she pulled on some jogging pants and a white T-shirt with a sketch of a human brain on it and the words "There isn't an app for this." Nice.

Kit looked at me again and started toward my bed, eyeing it like a hawk eyes its prey.

I moved to deflect her and defend my territory, what pitiful little there was of it.

Her face scrunched up in a grimace and she changed course. "Why does everyone have to be so messy?" she asked. I don't think she expected an answer. We certainly didn't give her one.

Kit wrung her hands. "And what kind of a name is Cordi?" she said, her voice almost curdling over the word. "Sounds like an electrical device." Must be a heavy sleeper, I thought, to have missed my explanation.

Mavis was practically bursting a stitch to answer Kit's question, so I let her. It seemed to satisfy Kit and she turned to her little chest of drawers, before pulling out a neatly folded blouse and pants. It took a while for her to get dressed. Mavis had been much faster. Lucy, too. She'd dumped her PJs on the bed, changed into hot-pink sweats, yanked on hot-pink running shoes, and left.

I thought about just leaving for breakfast without Kit and Mavis, but I didn't have the nerve to go there all by myself, so I waited. I had a vague recollection of my meals being brought to me in whatever room I had had before this one, but I wasn't sure, and I had no memory of any cafeteria or wherever it was that we ate.

Kit became obsessed with the creases on her blouse that she couldn't get rid of, and it made her cry, until Mavis took her by the hand and led her to the door. Kit glanced back at me as I rose from my bed, and then she gripped the door handle and opened it. I was right on Mavis's tail and almost bumped into her when, for no apparent reason, Kit shut the door and stopped our forward momentum. I looked at Mavis, but she only smiled vacantly as Kit opened and closed the door nine times before finally entering the hallway.

chapter three

I f you have ever walked down a long hospital corridor, then you know the fear and dread it can inspire, as well as the hope. I was getting a bit of each as I walked down the tiled floors past the rows of doors to patient rooms, under the institutional lighting and the institutional pale green paint of the walls and the white ceiling tiles with little dark specks floating in them. All hospitals seemed to have those little dark specks floating in their ceilings.

I was feeling overwhelmed and I followed Mavis like a dog its master as we passed by the nurses' station. It was a self-enclosed area with three of its four walls a row of sectioned glass panels from the waist up, so that anybody could see in at any time. From the waist down it was solid wall. One of the sectioned glass panels had a window through which we could speak to the nurses without their having to open the heavy door into the station. There was an identical window in the wall facing the lobby where the elevators were, and one on the far side, where Mavis told me the men had their rooms.

The station itself was crammed with desks and computers and stacks of paperwork. I could see Ella sitting at a computer while another nurse hovered over her, pointing something out on the screen. The cafeteria was just past the nursing station and the door from the lobby, and I almost bolted when I saw how many people were sitting down eating.

I counted six, not including my contingent, but viewed from my state of mind, it might as well have been a hundred. I looked around for Kit, but she was still halfway back down the hall. She was jumping from tile to tile, meticulously avoiding all the lines, her face set in a grimace of determination. At that rate she'd be another five minutes.

So I followed Mavis up to the counter and ordered some toast and some wizened-looking blueberries for my breakfast. The woman behind the counter looked as though she hadn't slept in years. The bags under her eyes would have held all my groceries for a week. She tried to entice me to take some scrambled eggs, or at least some cheese for my protein, but my stomach turned at the mere mention of either.

Mavis took her tray and went to sit with Lucy and a chubby guy who looked to be about thirty. Two other tables were full and I looked across, enviously, at two young men, each sitting alone at a table. I thought for a moment of doing the same thing, but it would make a statement I wasn't sure was a good one to make, so instead I plunked my tray down beside Mavis and sat. She introduced me to the chubby guy, Austin, who barely acknowledged me. He appeared to be listening intently to Lucy, who was talking a blue streak. I noticed Austin's pale grey-blue eyes and cute little nose and thought he could once have been a teacher's pet. His light-brown wispy hair was thinning, so maybe he was older than thirty.

Lucy was speaking so fast I could barely get the gist. But in some odd way she and Austin seemed to understand each other perfectly, because the lopsided conversation continued, or maybe they didn't understand each other at all, but were simply reacting to the sound of each other's voices. Even my arrival, then Kit's, didn't interrupt Lucy's flow. At last I picked up some of what she was saying — she had just decided that she was going to run for Parliament in the next election and that she would then save all the forests from destruction and turn the oil sands into an environmental oasis. She sounded excited and sure of herself, until Austin told her that all politicians were out to get us and why would she be any different? She hesitated and then told him to shut up and mind his own business. Things were silent after that, for a while. But then Lucy started up again about running for Parliament and I tuned out.

I looked over at the two solitary men. One was furiously writing in a notebook and eating at the same time. He had long black hair and a beard trying hard to be a beard and failing miserably. His eyes were watery and anemic-looking in a long pale face that looked as if it had been rolled and stretched out with a rolling pin, with an aquiline nose stuck on as an afterthought. It was a face that looked young and vulnerable — he couldn't have been more than nineteen — made somehow more so by the dimple in his cheek. He was still wearing navy-blue pajamas that poked out from under a shabby burgundy dressing gown.

Mavis saw the direction of my gaze and said, "That's Bradley. Sometimes he doesn't talk at all, and he keeps pretty much to himself. He doesn't like people very much."

We both stared at Bradley, who seemed oblivious, as he made notes in his book.

"He went off his meds, and with schizophrenia you can't do that. Not with *any* mental illness. I know. I tried."

And Mavis giggled her little-girl giggle, but I saw no giggle in her eyes. I wondered what kind of problems she had harboured before her medication had kicked in, although I vaguely remembered her saying someone was stealing her, so maybe her meds still needed to be tweaked. Probably why she was here.

"Bradley's much better since he came in and they put him on new meds, but he's still not right." She sighed. "I guess we're all still not right. That's why we're here. At least we aren't the sickest, though; at least we don't pose a security threat." I looked at her in some alarm. "We're not violent. They live on another floor."

Mavis said the second man was Leo. He was tall, with his knees bunched up under the table, and he was painfully skinny. His clothes hung from his sloping shoulders, valiantly trying to find some part of him to hold them up. His face was flaccid and splotchy and his eyes were sunken, so that he looked a bit like a raccoon. He was eating his food without taking his eyes off any of us. I noticed he had taken the chair closest to the wall and was sitting on the edge of the seat, as if ready for flight. I caught his eye and he quickly looked away, as if I had intruded on him by just looking at him.

Suddenly someone called Mavis's name. She swivelled to look and I followed her gaze just in time to see Bradley incline his head at her. She looked around and caught my eye, and something in the vagueness of her gaze made me quickly look away as she got up and went over to Bradley's table. He was holding something out for her in his hand and she hesitated, looking over her shoulder at me before hastily taking it from him and putting it in her pocket. For someone who didn't like people, it seemed like an odd thing for Bradley to do.

She came back to me with an uncertain smile and said, "He's always giving me candy," but she wouldn't meet my eyes.

We were sitting at one of seven tables set at right angles to the bank of cafeteria windows, so that we couldn't actually look outside without turning our heads. To the right of the windows was a door painted the cheery colour of a canary and plastered with the words NO ADMITTANCE. One *t* was missing and someone had added the letter with a red Magic Marker. As I was looking at it, the door opened and out walked a man with a shock of white hair. I vaguely remembered him trying to get me to agree to something, but I couldn't remember what. Without the overpowering drag of the fog on my mind I realized that he was my doctor. I remembered thinking that he was as old as the hills when I first met him. I revised my observation now to a prematurely grey forty-year-old.

Lucy, who had been getting more and more detailed about her future run for Parliament, fell silent when she saw the doctor. She dropped her head, but just before she did I caught a fleeting glimpse of something inexplicable on her face. Was it panic? But then Austin, whose back was to the doctor, told her that if she was running he was going to run in her riding, as well, and they would sit side by side in the legislature as Liberal MPs, as if he had totally forgotten his distaste for politicians. Lucy forgot about the doctor in her eagerness to answer Austin. What was weird was that it didn't seem to occur to either of them that they couldn't both run for the same seat and win. I had the smug little thought that I had actually noticed, sick as I was.

The doctor stopped at the end of the table and surveyed us like a kindergarten class. He was wearing a nametag that pegged him as Dr. Osborn — no first name — pinned to the traditional white lab coat many doctors preferred. He had a handsome rough-hewn face with high cheekbones, pockmarked with the scars of teenage acne. Close up, his hair was like snow, white and deep and thick.

"Mavis. It's time." His voice was gentle, reassuring. Everybody at the table stared for a second, including me. Then Austin pushed his chair away from the table and Mavis sidled closer to me. She looked up at Dr. Osborn, sideways, a frown creasing her entire forehead. Finally she found part of her voice.

"For what?" she asked, pathetically, because of course she knew.

"Your ECT," he said, making it sound like it was a soothing massage or something.

"But it's Lucy's turn," she said.

"Have you forgotten, Mavis?" he said gently. "I reminded you several times yesterday."

Mavis looked confused. She struggled to say something, but would not meet Osborn's gaze.

"I don't want it," she said in a barely discernible whisper.

"Let's just go and talk about it then," he said. I looked at Mavis and back at Dr. Osborn and wondered if I'd told him all my secrets. Surely not.

Mavis suddenly leaped up from the table as if she'd been bitten. Unable to help, I watched as her tray flipped up and crashed against her, before falling to the floor, leaving a blaze of red cranberry juice on her white T-shirt with the brain emblazoned on it.

"Oh, no!" she said, her voice cracking. "It's my favourite." She frantically wiped at her shirt with a napkin.

"That's okay, Mavis," said Dr. Osborn. "One of the nurses will see that it gets cleaned." Mavis stared at him as if she thought he was lying and then, wiping her hand across her mouth, she knelt on the floor to pick up the tray.

"Let's go, Mavis," said Dr. Osborn. Mavis stood up with the tray and turned her gaze directly on me, and the mixture of emotions I saw there was a kaleidoscope of confusion, defiance, fear, resignation, excitement. Then she turned, dropped the tray on the table, jammed her hands into her pants' pockets and followed the doctor back through the NO ADMITTANCE door that admitted a Mavis who wished the sign meant what it said.

Meanwhile Kit had jumped up and was frantically wiping up the mess with a balled-up wad of napkins. We all just sat there and watched her. No one thought to offer to help.

"Poor sod," said Lucy as she stared absently after Mavis. "They steal a little more of you each time. For her own good, though, that's what they say. She'll wake up happy — she just won't know why." And she laughed, the haunting laughter of someone who knew.

Before I even thought about questioning her, a leonine colossus of a man slid his heavily laden tray one-handedly onto the tabletop as if it were a mere butterfly. He had what I call stage presence, a certain flamboyance. He smiled at me and flicked his blond mane out of a pair of startlingly green eyes as he sat with surprising grace. He was a real hunk of a man. I figured he must be about six foot five and well over two hundred pounds of pure muscle. He was clean-shaven and deeply tanned with high cheekbones and a strong Roman nose. His lips were smooth and just the right size for getting lost in.

"You finally woke up, eh?" he said. He pulled me out of my reverie and I started guiltily. I looked behind me.

"'You' being me?" I asked and he responded with a cat-got-the-mouse smile.

"I'm Cordi," I said and wished I were somewhere else, because there were too many people and my mind was too brittle and it was way too early in the morning to be thinking the thoughts I was thinking, or any thoughts at all, for that matter.

"Jacques, at your service," and he gestured with his hand to encompass the whole table. In doing so he knocked over his little plastic cup filled with orange juice — glass I guess was taboo — and annihilated my impression that he was graceful. Kit, who had finished with the floor and resumed sitting quietly, gasped and started mopping up the mess with her napkin, taking care to keep her hands from getting wet.

"Oh, for Christ's sake, get your hands off my tray," said Jacques, who then had the good sense to look sheepish.

Kit's hand fluttered around the tray like an injured bird, until Lucy pulled her away.

I thought it might be a good idea to change the topic and give Kit a chance to collect herself. "What's wrong with Mavis?" I asked, point-blank. Kit inhaled sharply and looked away from me. Lucy looked stunned and Jacques looked amused.

"We're not supposed to say," said Lucy.

I waited, but it was no good. Lucy may have known, but she wasn't saying. Jacques said impatiently, "Oh, for Christ's sakes. She's schizophrenic." He looked at me, his green eyes lucid and clear, making me feel flustered in a way that wasn't all bad. Not all bad at all.

But then he spoiled it by asking, "Is that what you are?" As if my diagnosis, whatever it was, defined who I was.

I wasn't up to this. I looked away and said nothing.

"Still in the denial phase, eh?" He was so persistent! I wondered if he was always like this.

Lucy came to my rescue. "Just because *you're* still denying that you're ill doesn't mean she is."

"I didn't say that, did I? And I'm not in denial. Never have been," and he lifted his little orange juice container as if to say "Cheers."

"You're definitely in denial if you're denying you have a problem with alcohol," said Lucy impatiently.

"Said like a true manic-depressive."

"What's that supposed to mean?" Lucy pushed back her chair and stood, her face flushed.

"Don't get your knickers in a knot. It's just a saying."

"Well, don't say it anymore." Lucy picked up her tray. "And besides, don't you know anything? It's bipolar disorder, not manic depression anymore." She left without looking at Jacques, who shrugged and winked at me.

"One week she's manic as hell and the next she's depressed," said Jacques. He wasn't expecting me to answer, but even I knew they had changed the name, partly because of the stigma associated with it.

"Hence manic depression," he added, emphasizing both words by drawing them out. "Does bipolar say as much?"

Breakfast had exhausted me. I left Kit counting tiles in the hall and went back to bed.

I lay there, prisoner of the fog and the anxiety, or whatever the hell it was, washing over me, and the awful sense of foreboding that something was going to go wrong. It haunted me, because what more than my broken mind could go wrong with me here?

I was lying there, looking at the speckled ceiling tiles, when there was a gentle knock on the door and Ella walked in.

"Dr. Osborn is free to see you now," she said.

She looked at my quizzical face and said, "We don't make set appointments here. We just come and get you when the doctor's ready."

I realized what a different culture it was in here from that outside in the real world, one where the patient didn't have to wait, one where all the responsibilities of the world were checked at the front door, and one where demons were wrestled into checkmate by patients and doctors alike. It was a comfortable feeling, a cocooning feeling.

Ella led me down the hall to the cafeteria and the door that said NO ADMITTANCE. On the other side it was somehow anticlimactic — just an ordinary hallway with office entrances on one side, the other side being the mutual wall with the cafeteria. But they weren't all just offices, as I discovered when we passed an open door and I looked in. I saw one bed and a lot of medical equipment that took up most of the room.

When I looked more closely I could see a pair of purple-and-yellow running shoes tucked under the bed. So this was where Mavis had come. Something about the room seemed familiar to me, but I couldn't place it. Had I been there before? I felt a queer sensation, almost as if my mind was sliding on ice and couldn't get a grip. *What was that all about?* I wondered.

I followed Ella down the hall, turned a corner, and watched as she knocked on a door. I heard a muffled "Come in," and she opened the door and gestured for me to go inside.

I did so and immediately got lost. The grass-green rug on the floor, speckled with darker green swirls, was at least two inches thick, and I sank into it like a thick carpet of moss. All four walls and the ceiling were covered in photos of what appeared to be a West Coast forest, the towering trees of another era transplanted into an office the size of half a tennis court. As I closed the door behind me all the outside noises disappeared, cut off with the finality of a guillotine, almost as if the room was sound proofed. Dr. Osborn was sitting at a large wooden desk, talking softly on the phone. He looked up as I walked in and smiled.

I stood uncertainly for a moment, the odd silence unnerving me, when he motioned me to the sofa in the middle of the room. By the soft mellow light of a floor lamp I could see that there were no windows or, if there had been, they'd been blocked out. The sofa was forest-green leather and matched an armchair pulled up close to it. Beyond the sofa was his desk with computers and filing cabinets and a stereo system. As I sat down on one end of the sofa, close to an arm and as far away from the chair as I could get, the room suddenly filled with the soft sounds of rain falling through a forest to the needled ground below.

"Do you mind the music?" he asked as he hung up and came and sat down in the chair, seemingly oblivious to how I had distanced myself from him, out of some need to hold myself together and not let him see how vulnerable I was. Stupid really, but I don't talk about myself easily.

"It's nice," I said.

He smiled. "When I was a boy and had nightmares and couldn't sleep, my mother would play this for me."

"It doesn't put you to sleep anymore?" I asked, wondering how he could deal with patients without dozing off.

He laughed, but didn't say anything. Instead he looked at me for a moment and then said, "How are you, Cordi?"

I took a deep breath. "I've been better," I said lightly.

"You've been through a horrible depression. No one should have to go through what you have gone through. But you did. What do you remember of it?"

I sat there, feeling myself clamming up.

"You don't have to tell me anything, Cordi. You know that, don't you?"

I nodded.

"It helps sometimes, though. To talk. If only to know that someone else knows and sympathizes. I can help you, Cordi."

I looked at him sitting there, the concern in his face genuine. We sat in silence for some moments, listening to the rain, until I finally said, "I remember sleeping. I couldn't get up. I remember my brother cajoling me to eat, pleading with me, and I felt like I was outside of my own body, watching all this and wanting to respond. But I couldn't. I couldn't even hug my brother when he started to cry." I couldn't believe I'd just revealed that, but Osborn somehow made it easy to talk. Or maybe it was the rain and the trees and the feeling of being in a womb.

"And how did that make you feel?"

"It made me feel like nobody, that I didn't exist anymore."

"Were you aware you were ill?" he said.

"I knew something wasn't right."

"Then you knew you were in a clinical depression."

"It doesn't work like that," I said.

"What do you mean?"

"The emptiness destroys all your feelings. It takes over everything, the will to live, the will to eat, the will to love, the will to help yourself. It leaves nothing behind, so there's no understanding, no knowledge that I was in a clinical depression. Even if I'd had that knowledge, it wouldn't have mattered. The depression or emptiness itself makes sure of that. It comes unbidden and for no reason. You must know that."

He looked at me and sighed. "I just wanted to hear it in your words." There was silence then, but I had nothing further to say. After a while he finally spoke. "Do you remember your brother bringing you here?"

I nodded. "Some of it is a blur, though."

"How much do you remember from the time you entered hospital until today?" he asked.

He was being awfully insistent. Hadn't we covered this already? "Bits and pieces," I finally said.

"Does anything stand out?"

"Not really. I guess I must have slept most of the time?"

Osborn nodded. "Yes. You did a lot of that. And the medications would have made you sleepy, but you seem to have forgotten a lot. Do you remember me?" He certainly was interested in my memory.

"Vaguely."

"I was the doctor who admitted you." He paused. "Perhaps we need to adjust your medication." He said it more to himself than to me, as I watched his mind turning over the problem of me and my meds. It felt encouraging to see someone taking it all so seriously. Serious in my context surely meant getting better.

We talked a bit more and he said he was "guardedly encouraged" about my progress, that the depression was dissipating, but he wanted to keep an eye on me for a while longer, and then he showed me to the door, the glaring lights of the hall making me recoil and want to go back into his office, where it felt safe and warm and separate from the outside world.

I was exhausted and went back to my empty room and curled up on my bed and fell asleep. I was woken by a cluster of people crowding into our room. Mavis had come back from her ECT and was looking a little dozy. Kit and Ella were hovering around her like bees around the queen. I sat up in bed, feeling really really groggy and watched as Mavis spied her clean white T-shirt on her bed. She held it up in shaky hands so I could see the outline of the brain and read the slogan, and she said, "The red cranberry juice came out," to no one in particular.

Lucy, who had come into the room on Mavis's heels, looked at her in some confusion, opened her mouth to say something, and then apparently thought better of it. Even in my wiped-out state I knew that something was going on. I just didn't know what.

chapter four

When I awoke the next morning Kit and Lucy had already left, presumably to take showers. Only 8:05. Ten minutes before breakfast. I rolled over and saw Mavis's arm hanging over the edge of her bed, my mind taking a while to process the weird way her arm was hanging. I sat up and took a better look. Her arm was flopped over the bed so that her hand was dragging on the floor, and when I looked more closely I could see the outline of her head, hidden under the covers, angled in a way that sent shivers down my spine. I got out of bed and padded over to her, softly calling her name. There was no response. Gingerly I crept closer and tapped her on the arm with one finger. She didn't move and her arm seemed cold to the touch. I reached over and pulled back the covers. And gasped.

Her face was grey, lifeless, erased in a tableau of death, a long crimson scarf wound around her neck. I stood there, frozen, scared, my heart racing. I knew the face of death and she was wearing it. I shuddered, one long convulsive shiver. She had died inches away from me, her life ebbing out as I lay sleeping. Had my meds made me sleep that soundly? I hastily covered her face. I suddenly wanted to get the hell out of there. And so I ran out into the hall to look for help.

I could see Jacques lounging against the wall near the one pay phone we were allowed to use. He had what looked like a pencil hanging out of his mouth — a surrogate cigarette maybe? He was addicted to alcohol, so why not cigarettes? Farther down, near the room where the nurses usually dispensed our meds, was a row of chairs where we waited each night for the pills that kept us sane, at least more or less. Austin was sitting in the closest chair, head down and talking to himself. Kit and Leo were there, too, Kit sitting primly in the second chair, her hands in her lap. Leo sat apart from them, balanced once again on the edge of his chair. Lucy was pacing the hall like a caged tiger. It was too early for meds. Were they all waiting for breakfast? I could smell the tantalizing aroma of bacon even from where I stood. Question answered.

And then I caught sight of Ella as she entered the corridor from one of the bedrooms and started walking away from us all. I called out and watched as Jacques, Lucy and Austin, Kit and Leo all swivelled to look from her to me. Ella turned and hesitated, and then called out that she'd be back in a while. It was a pretty public place to be having a conversation, but I didn't want to wait a while, so I said in a loud voice, "This can't wait."

Ella hesitated and then, not bothering to hide her annoyance, came down the corridor toward me. Even in my distress I could not help but notice the seductive way she walked, seemingly oblivious to the way she carried herself, her hips swinging rhythmically to and fro.

"Mavis's dead," I said without preamble.

Anywhere else such a statement would have raised an alarm, but Ella stared at me and said, "Now, dear, did you take your meds last night?" She knew I had, of course. The nurses were under orders to watch you swallow them.

When I didn't answer, she said, "I'm sure you just had a bad dream," and she turned to go. I watched her walking back down the corridor toward Lucy and the others and I let it rip in the loudest voice I could manage.

"MAVIS IS DEAD." The words sounded as stark and cold as Mavis herself.

Ella stopped in her tracks. There was a long period of silence and then, inexplicably, Austin said, "Of course she's dead. She was murdered."

I felt this cold creepy little thing crawl up my spine. What the hell did he mean by that? And then it occurred to me that maybe he was psychotic or something and was acting up, which immediately made me realize I was no better than Ella, who assumed my illness was making me see things. Leo stood up and yelled that we were all unsafe, and the fear plastered across his face belied his name. Ella came back down the corridor. She tried to calm Leo down before dealing with me, but he seemed to be in an awful panic and she had to talk him down as I waited. As we all waited. After some minutes another nurse arrived and took Leo under her care. Ella was struggling with controlling her temper, as she came and took me by the arm and propelled me into my room.

"Cordi, you must learn to control what you say. You'll just rile everybody up and scare people. Leo doesn't need this."

"In the meantime," I said, "would you try to wake up Mavis for me please? She's late for breakfast." Mean, but effective, and it was not an unreasonable request.

Ella turned and walked over to Mavis's bed and called out her name, the same way I had.

"She's not going to hear you," I said helpfully.

Ella glanced at me, but her attention was now squarely on Mavis. She shook her by the shoulder and when nothing happened she pulled off the sheets and jumped back.

"Mavis is dead!" she said, her voice pockmarked with surprise. But then she gathered herself together and reached over to feel for a pulse. There was a long silence and then she surprised the hell out of me. "She's still alive," said Ella as our eyes met in that no man's land of confusion, suspicion, and subterfuge.

Ella hustled me out of my room faster than I normally run and told me that under no circumstances was I to go back in. Then she ran down the corridor to the nursing station, stumbling at the door before disappearing inside and immediately returning with some reinforcements. The group rushed into my room, while I stood there, in the middle of the corridor, under the glaring lights, with five pairs of eyes glued on me. I could see them there, just down the hall, but I felt removed from them, on the outside of my mind, looking in. I could see their mouths moving, but no sound reached my ears. I was like a person in the fog, all senses dulled, all thoughts distorted and fractured. Nothing was sharp. Nothing was clear. Everything was foggy and I felt an enormous wave of hopelessness rush through me.

I started to turn away, but Jacques called out, "Not on your life, girl. Spill it."

I looked at them all looking at me and thought that the world sometimes seemed like a very small place. These people were my world right now. I had to live with them. I started walking down the corridor toward them.

"I thought she was dead," I said.

"Is she? So how did she die, Cordi?" Lucy asked. "Did she die in bed?"

"What did she look like?" This from Austin.

"Did she suffer?" Now Lucy.

"Did she hang herself?" Jacques.

"Was it contagious?" Leo.

Ghoulish, yes, but all questions that death brings out in people as they try to grasp the loss of a life, especially of one so young. But none of them seemed to have heard what I said. They were all stuck on what I had first said, that Mavis was dead. I realized they were all looking for different answers. Jacques, for instance, I imagined wanted to hear that she hung herself inexpertly and her face was contorted in death. Lucy might want to hear that she died peacefully in her sleep, Austin that some sinister force had carried her away. And Leo? I didn't know what to think about Leo. At least he seemed to have calmed down.

So all I told them again was that she actually hadn't died. At least that was what Ella had said. But I was uneasy. When our eyes had met, hers had said something altogether different.

They peppered me with more questions after that, but I just shrugged and walked away as several more medical personnel moved quickly down the corridor. I turned and watched them go into my room and wondered if I'd have the same room come nightfall. Would they put me and Lucy and Kit in a dead woman's room? But then I had to remind myself that she wasn't dead. And it was a hospital, after all. Beds went empty all the time and had to be filled with the next in line. No time for sensitivities.

And that was when I heard an unholy moan welling up like some monstrous ululation. I turned and saw Leo, his raccoon eyes wild in a panic that consumed his whole body. He was gasping for air, like a fish out of water, and his face was the colour of chalk, but glistened like a snake. He seemed to be battling a fear all his own, as though something had caught him by the throat and was hanging on until death. I watched as his skinny legs slid out from under him and he crumpled to the floor like a skeleton, his breaths coming jerky and jagged.

"I'm going to die," he croaked, the words sounding like a sword had been thrust into his heart.

I was the closest to him and by the time I had loosened his shirt, the same nurse who had helped him before knelt down beside him and took his pulse. He had further unnerved me and I was feeling a little ill.

"I'm going to die," Leo said again. "I'm having a heart attack!" His voice was wild with fear, his frightened sunken eyes beseeching the nurse, who was trying to calm him, but it was like trying to talk a moth from the flame.

Leo's fear was contagious. I felt it crawling up my spine, and when I looked up and saw Jacques and Austin, I saw fear reflected in their faces. But the nurse was calm, matter of fact, weirdly so, as if this wild thing that was happening was as harmless as a rabbit. She told Leo to breathe deeply and began counting the breaths for him. He looked like hell and I wondered why the nurse hadn't called for the doctor. Maybe he *was* having a heart attack. But no, the nurse continued to talk to him in soothing tones for about five minutes, and Leo seemed to revive enough for the nurse to get him on his feet and walk him to his room.

Lucy was standing in the hallway near where Leo had been, her eyes stitched wide, unsure of what had just happened.

"Did you see that?" she asked.

I was unable or unwilling to talk to her. Maybe both.

"I've never seen a panic attack before, have you?"

I stared at Lucy, my mind wrapping itself around Leo's illness. I shook my head and turned my back on her. I didn't feel like talking. In truth I was shaken. So many people with so many problems. It seemed insurmountable.

Immediately after Leo's panic attack, the powers that be rounded us all up and herded us into the cafeteria, where we were given a very brief announcement that someone had taken ill and we were to stay in the cafeteria, or the north wing of the unit, while they dealt with the situation. The south wing and all rooms were out of bounds.

The patients had coalesced into small groups that had congregated around the tables, but I didn't feel like joining any of them. There was only one other table left and it was occupied by Bradley, the guy in his late teens who sat staring into space, a vacant look on his scary-pale face.

Up close his scraggly black beard looked a little more robust than it did from a distance. I pulled my chair up and said hello, but he didn't respond. Not even his eyes blinked. He seemed so vulnerable, so young, too young to be here.

"He won't be talking to you," Jacques said in a deeply soothing voice. He was leaning back against the next table.

"Bradley doesn't talk much," he added. Mavis had said something similar to me. "He's schizophrenic. Lives in his own world most of the time."

Just like Mavis, I thought. I thought back to the interaction Bradley had had with Mavis, trying to remember if he had talked. He had certainly interacted.

I looked back at Bradley, hoping Jacques would leave me alone and hoping he wouldn't. He intrigued me.

"I guess you've never seen a dead person before, eh?"

I didn't feel the need to respond to that.

"But you got it wrong," he added.

I must have involuntarily tensed my face or something, because he said, "You didn't get it wrong?" The emphasis was on *didn't*.

He went on, "You were there first. You saw her. Is she dead or not?" I looked at Jacques more closely then. His voice was so insistent.

"I thought she was, but I'm not a nurse, and the nurse said she wasn't dead," I replied reluctantly.

"Typical," he said.

"What do you mean by that?" I said defensively.

"Well, would you want to tell a bunch of potentially suicidal patients that someone had succeeded in offing themselves right under their noses?"

I hadn't seen that coming. "You mean she lied to me?"

"Easier than facing the music with us."

"Yeah, but I'd already yelled out that she was dead," I said, intrigued by his theory nonetheless.

He smiled. "You're a patient. Who's going to believe you?" The look in his eyes was difficult to fathom, like deep bottomless pools hiding the unknown. It was disconcerting.

"Which leaves us with the question of how she died, if she died," he said with a flourish of his hand. "Was there anything suspicious about her death, that is, if she *is* dead?" He seemed unable or unwilling to keep the drama out of his voice.

"What do you mean by 'suspicious'?" I could feel a pang of distinct unease steal over me, along with a quiver of interest. It was actually a good moment for me, to feel interest in something, even if it was so negative and fleeting. And suddenly it occurred to me that maybe Leo was right and she'd died of some contagious disease, and they were covering it up. And that made me very anxious and very scared. I didn't want to die and I knew this awful feeling would never go away until I learned the truth about Mavis.

Jacques laughed and turned away from me, but as he did so he said playfully, "What if Austin's right? That she was murdered? That is, if she really did die." It was a devil's advocate sort of thing to say. Which made me even more anxious.

That and the scarf around her neck.

I stared at him then, not able to capture the urge to engage him over that last question, even though it alarmed me. I mean, why would anyone want to murder Mavis? Why would Austin have even said that? Did he know something I didn't?

Jacques smiled and then pushed away from the table and left me alone with Bradley. I watched him go, his easy fluid gait making me think of a lion on the prowl. I turned back to Bradley, pulled my chair closer, and cradled my head in my hands, mimicking his posture. She was dead. I knew it. I had seen her.

On a whim I said, "I found her," keeping my voice low. Bradley stared at me blankly.

"She was lying with her arm dangling." Bradley seemed to be in another world, not taking in anything I said, and I found I needed to say a lot to someone who would not repeat my fears.

"Her face was so grey, so gone, so not there anymore. It scared me because it hit like a punch to the gut that youth is no antidote to dying. Do you know what I mean? So why are they saying she's not dead? I know what I saw and what I saw was death. So why are they hiding it?"

I looked at Bradley and saw myself in the darkness he was inhabiting and I shivered, because the tendrils of that evil place were still willowing inside me. Would Bradley ever emerge? Maybe Mavis had been depressed and maybe she hadn't emerged. But she hadn't seemed depressed. Maybe she had hidden it and had killed herself somehow with the scarf, the blackness of mental illness so full of death and despair and its victims often so fatally good at hiding it. Poor Mavis would become just another statistic. Or so I thought at the time.

My inertia came in waves, so that in between I was able to operate more or less normally. Which was how I realized that I had not used the washroom since the night before and had to go really badly, but we were still confined to the cafeteria. The problem was that the women's washroom was on the corridor right across from where Mavis lay. All the patients were clustered in the cafeteria and there were no nurses in sight. I looked down the corridor and saw no one, so I loped down and ducked into the washroom. I was still trying to get Mavis's death face out of my mind, but I was failing miserably.

On my way back to the cafeteria I got a clear view of my room. They had Mavis on a gurney, her crossword PJs a taunting reminder of the life they had once held, her crimson scarf wrapped around her neck as if she had been tossing and turning. The sight of her ashen face, eyes and mouth now closed, made me gasp. Mavis's helpers turned around at the sound, including Ella and Dr. Osborn, who'd been hovering over the body.

Ella hastily grabbed me by the arm and thrust me ahead of her and down the hall, without saying a word. I turned once to look behind me and saw Dr. Osborn staring after me, a look of sadness, and something else, flickering across his face. Even in my confusion over their cover-up, it made me wonder how nurses and doctors do it, how they manage to cope with so much pain and death. Osborn's look made me realize that sometimes they didn't. And it made me realize to what extremes they will go to protect their living patients. Like getting Mavis's body to the morgue without anyone on the floor realizing she was dead.

Except I knew.

And because I knew I couldn't stop thinking about her. How had the scarf got there in the first place? There were definite rules on the floor. There were no blinds in our room, no lamps with cords, the TV was covered in Plexiglas — its cord was run through a plastic tube — we ate with plastic cutlery, drank from plastic cups, no glass, and we had to check in with the nurses if we brought anything onto the floor that could be used for self-harm, including computer and cellphone powercords.

Was Austin right? Could it have been murder? And if so, why?

chapter five

Mavis didn't come back and her bed remained empty. It had been Austin's thin insistent voice that had got me to thinking about murder as a definite possibility, that and Jacques. I mean, why not? It can occur anywhere, with anyone, at any time. And I could still see the scarf wound around her neck. Could she have accidentally strangled herself? Surely not. She would have awakened. And so would we. Or maybe not. The drugs I was on could put a horse to sleep. Maybe it was the same for Lucy and Kit. Suicide was more likely, but if it was murder or some awful disease, I needed to protect myself so that I didn't become the next victim. And in order to do that, I needed to find out what had happened. How had she died?

I felt a quickening in my brain and a surge of energy. I sought out Austin. He was slouched down in the saggy old sofa in the common room, which was open concept with the cafeteria. He had managed to monopolize a weak little shred of sunlight that was sneaking through the winter-stained window onto the couch. His chubby face was tilted up into it as if he was trying to get a tan. When I sat down beside him he looked over at me, but there was no real interest in his face, just a slightly vacuous look. I wondered why he was here at the hospital, what was wrong with him. He repositioned himself in the sunbeam.

"Do you remember earlier when you said Mavis had been murdered?" I asked.

He glanced at me again, and again looked away.

"What did you mean?" I said.

He had closed his eyes and was resting his fledgling double chin on his neck, in the pose of a man getting ready to sleep. I was frustrated and was about to prod him again when he said, "Aren't we all murder victims?" Which sounded like a non sequitur and a cop-out to me, and didn't appease my frustration one iota.

"But you said she was murdered," I persisted. "Who murdered her?"

He laughed a snarky little laugh and said, without once opening his eyes, "People take over our minds and souls all the time. Politicians, doctors, journalists, nurses. They twist our minds to their liking. If that isn't murder I don't know what is. Mavis was infected by them." Suddenly he opened his eyes and stared right at me, but it felt as though he was looking right through me.

"Did she show you the article they wrote about her?" he asked.

I shook my head. He ran his hands through what little hair he had and said, "It was all about split personalities, even though she stressed that that is not what schizophrenia is. We are not Dr. Jekyll and Mr. Hyde.

We sometimes argue with perfect fluidity from the wrong premise, making it sound believable, if you believe the premise. Ours may be a false reality. But it's real to us, even if it's false to everyone else."

Austin was an enigma playing out his own scenario. Based on the premise that politicians and doctors can manipulate people, he seemed believable, but the premise that manipulation means murder was a little hard to swallow. Still, almost reasonable and I wondered if this was because his meds were working. But then I remembered that just the other day he had plotted with Lucy to become a politician and win the same seat.

I knew I was out of my league with Austin. I didn't really know what I was dealing with. My only knowledge of mental illness came from reading books and from my own depression. So I was in the dark in more ways than one. And I really wanted to find an answer to the problem that was Mavis.

"So you don't know exactly who murdered her?" I asked.

He just sat there and stared at me, his forefinger beating out a rhythm on his pudgy knee.

I tried a different tack. "Did you like Mavis?"

"You mean, did Mavis like me," he said.

I felt as though we were talking around each other, like two circling boxers, but just what we were circling around I had no idea. He had turned away from me and had picked up a motorcycle magazine. I thought about trying to continue the conversation, but decided against it. His murderers were all in his head.

I thought about Mavis and how she had been spirited off the ward, and I even found myself doubting my own eyes. I had seen her, not once, but twice, in death, hadn't I? Murder or suicide, she was dead. But why had no police come to interview us? I feared that a successful cover-up would mean her death would go unnoticed and someone else might die. I figured I owed it to her and to all of life's lost to get to the bottom of it. Just how I was going to go about doing that I wasn't sure, but I felt I had been given a new lease on life, and I felt stronger than I had in months.

Because suddenly I had a purpose.

The nurses, in their daily talks with me, had suggested I attend some of the classes set up for patients to help them cope. I hadn't wanted to go and no one was forcing me, but suddenly I was interested. Perhaps I could find some answers to Mavis. I left Austin and went and sat in on a CBT class — I knew the letters stood for "Cognitive Behavioural Therapy" — and it was a class that had been postponed a couple of hours because of Mavis. I had seen such classes on TV, of course, where you talk about what's bothering you and find out ways to prevent it from consuming you, ways to see how your thinking has been distorted. Lots of them were touchy-feely sessions that left me feeling uncomfortable at how the public probing of a mind can seem like a violation. But CBT was goal-oriented and problem-focused, or at least, that was what I had read in the course description Ella had dropped on my bed, so I had high hopes. You were allowed to choose what classes to take, but once you were with a group, you stayed with that group.

There were only seven other people in the group, including the instructor, which increased the chances of my having to participate, so I started to leave. But the instructor would have none of it. He was a nondescript man with a bland, clean-shaven face that would get lost in a crowd. There was nothing unusual about him except his age. From the deep creases on his face, he looked eighty, but the energetic way he walked around the classroom pegged him at about sixty or younger. He deftly held out a chair for me and asked me to sit. What could I do? I realized with some dismay that the class had already started, so I sat. Austin made me feel much better when he made a later appearance than I had and took his time finding a seat.

We were in a large, square room with a mishmash of sofas, institutional-type metal chairs, and tables of various heights and designs, along with a bunch of yoga mats and a treadmill. It was obviously a room shared by many different instructors, who moulded the room to their specific needs. Our instructor had chosen the sofa as a focal point and everyone had pulled up a chair of some description to inscribe a circle, more or less. Lucy and Kit were there, sitting side by side on the sofa, leaning into each other. Jacques and Austin sat beside each other in two armchairs, leaning away, and Bradley sat alone with two empty chairs on either side of him. Leo was perched on a chair closest to the door. There were two other people I didn't know, although I had seen them in the cafeteria. For my and Austin's benefit the instructor introduced himself as Joe and asked us our names.

He then pointed to his whiteboard and said, "Jacques has identified a situation where he lost his temper when his ex-wife used his alcoholism as a reason to get her sole custody of their children, while trying to get more financial support from him. That it has left him feeling guilty, afraid, frustrated, but mostly angry."

It actually made me feel quite good that Jacques wasn't married.

The instructor turned to Jacques and said, "Tell us what your automatic thoughts are? What first flashes through your mind about yourself and your situation?"

"That I hated her. That she didn't understand what an alcoholic has to go through to stop drinking. Unless you're a smoker or some other drug addict, it's impossible to know the depth of the loss when you quit. Try imagining having to give up your very favourite food — chocolate, steak, chips — and then multiply that unrequited hunger a hundred times over and you might feel something similar to what an alcoholic feels when faced with a future without alcohol."

The instructor waited for Jacques to say more but he didn't.

"Do you have any other automatic thoughts, besides hating your ex-wife?" It seemed kind of cold to just ignore most of what Jacques had just said, but maybe that was just part of the process, not to dwell on anyone's diagnosis.

"That our kids are not pawns. That she was taking me to the cleaners. I'd go bankrupt before paying her a cent."

"So of those three statements, which rankles the most? Which is the hot-button statement?"

Jacques thought about it for a moment, for actually quite a long moment, but finally he said, "That she was taking me to the cleaners and using the kids as pawns."

"Okay, let's look at the first one first, that she's taking you to the cleaners. How would you challenge that thought? Is it reasonable?"

"She *is* taking me to the cleaners."

"Do you think this is based on fact or an inaccurate perception based on how you feel?"

Jacques blinked.

"You need to challenge your negative thoughts. For example, there are laws preventing her from forcing you to pay more than you can. Do you think your anger at your ex-wife is getting in the way of rational thinking?"

Jacques scratched his head and didn't say anything, and the instructor did what every good psychiatrist and psychologist or social worker does — he let the silence flow around the room, waiting for Jacques to become uncomfortable and blurt something out. But Jacques remained silent and the instructor finally let it go by telling Jacques to think about it some more and that they would revisit his problem in another session. He then fixed me in his sights.

"What about you, Cordi? Can you tell us about a situation that has bothered you?" I was about to flat out say no when it suddenly occurred to me that maybe I could use the session to advantage.

"I saw Mavis dead in her bed." Everybody in the room snapped to attention.

"You mean you saw Mavis *sick* in her bed," prompted the instructor, who had obviously been briefed by someone.

"No, I meant what I said. I saw Mavis *dead* in her bed."

Joe looked around at the faces turned attentively toward him, and you could almost see his thoughts trying to get in line behind some strategy.

"Okay, Cordi. How did that make you feel?"

"Scared. Nauseated. Sad."

"And what thoughts went through your head when this happened?"

"That she was too young to die. Was it suicide? Was she murdered — because there was a scarf around her neck?"

"Is that all you felt and thought?" I nodded slowly and he said gently, "Perhaps you wondered if you were getting sick again."

I shook my head slowly, feeling the skin crawl on the back of my neck.

"What's your hot thought, the thought that means the most, Cordi?"

"That she died. That she was murdered."

He looked around at the others in the group, all of whom were leaning forward in their chairs.

"Okay. Let's go through a reasonable response to your thought. Do you have any proof to back up your claim?"

"The scarf, and the fact that scarves are not allowed on the floor."

"Perhaps a visitor left it behind," said Austin, who was squirming in his seat.

"But really, how do you strangle a person in a room with three other people in it?" asked Jacques.

"And how do you escape the attention of the nurses?" asked Leo.

"Maybe it was something else that killed her," said Kit.

I saw Austin stiffen at that and then he said, "Meaning?"

"I don't know," said Kit. "All I know is that, if she is dead, she didn't kill herself with a scarf." She sounded so sure that I wondered why.

"Be hard to strangle yourself with a scarf, unless you secured it to the ceiling," said Jacques dryly.

The instructor broke in and said, "Cordi, why do think she's dead?"

"I told you, I saw her," I said.

"But the nurses and doctors say otherwise."

"I think they're just trying to hide it from all of us, so we won't be traumatized by it."

"All I'm saying," said Joe gently, "is that I think you have to come to grips with the fact that your hot thought, that she is dead, might have been a simple misperception."

And that was the end of it for me. Not because we were through discussing my problem, but because Joe wanted to give someone else a chance to talk. Chicken.

chapter six

"Well, well, what have we here?"

I was sitting in the hall outside my room, head in hands, slumped against the wall. I didn't even bother to look up. I could tell by the gigantic feet that it was Jacques.

"Feeling sorry for ourselves, are we?" he said.

Even that didn't get my goat.

"Don't you even want to know what happened to her?"

That did get my goat. I looked up and said, "You know?"

"I didn't say that exactly."

"What *did* you say exactly?"

He squatted down beside me so that I didn't have to crane my neck. I was fascinated by the sheer size of his thighs as he did so. They were twice the size of mine and his hand, as he draped it over his knee, could have easily palmed my head.

"I'm curious, aren't you?" he said, his deep resonant voice bringing me back to the conversation at hand. "I'd like to know if she is dead or alive. If you are right or wrong. Purely academic."

"What did you have in mind, academically speaking?" I still had to look up at him, close enough to count some of the speckles in his lovely green eyes.

"Let's go to the morgue."

I wasn't sure I had heard him correctly. He repeated himself.

"Are you crazy?" I said.

Jacques smirked. "Can't you be more imaginative than that? We are, after all, in a psych hospital."

I felt two inches tall, but he had to rub it in.

"If I'm not crazy," he said, "then why am I here?" His voice was low, even, with a tinge of something indefinable hiding behind the amusement.

"Okay, okay. So you're crazy. But the morgue? Just how are we supposed to get there unobserved, assuming a psych hospital even has a morgue?" I asked.

"Oh, it has a morgue, and I know where it is."

"Is that all of your plan? Just go?" I said. And I really didn't want to know how he knew about the morgue. But he told me anyway.

He laughed. "I worked here once as a volunteer. The morgue isn't manned — they don't do autopsies here. It's just storage, so we have to go tonight, because if she's still there, they'll be moving her soon."

"And does working here once get you the key to get in?" I asked.

He laughed again and stood up and pulled out a jangly set of lock picks. He saw the surprised look on my face and said, "You've been here long enough, haven't you, to know that it's pretty easy to smuggle stuff onto the floor." Which begged the real questions of why he would want to smuggle in a set of picks in the first place and why he had them at all.

He was looking down, watching my face, which must have registered more surprise because he said, "Have you not signed out yet for a day pass or an overnight?"

I hadn't. Not because I didn't know about it — I knew I wasn't a prisoner — but because I was afraid to go back to my old life and find it lacking. Even stepping out onto the street left me feeling vaguely uneasy. Maybe just off the floor would be okay, though.

"So we just waltz out, zip down to the morgue, and unobserved, unlock the door, check for Mavis, and exit stage left?"

"You betcha."

It was some hours since Mavis had exited the floor on a stretcher, her body covered in a thin white sheet, the crimson scarf stuck like a leech to her neck. Cold crimson death. Jacques and I had agreed to sign out of the floor five minutes apart and right after dinner. He told me to take the elevator to the basement floor and he would be waiting for me. And so he was.

I stepped off the elevator and he took me by the arm and started walking down the long narrow corridor as if we were supposed to be there. His fingers on my skin were electric and I found myself thinking more about him than about what we were going to do. Then he let go and the moment was lost.

The lighting in the basement was budget-oriented and low-wattage, and cast more shadows than it dispersed. We came to a junction and he turned us to the right and we walked until we reached the end of the corridor. On the right-hand side was a maroon door conveniently labelled MORGUE. We were in an exposed position and I felt trapped, until I noticed the door across the way. It had a little window in it and I could see stairs going up. *If I'd missed that, the sign saying* STAIRS *would have alerted me*, I thought wryly.

While I was off in Neverland, Jacques was working wonders with his lock picks, and he nudged me with his massive paw when he got the door open. How the hell he had managed to work with the delicate locks with his big hands I couldn't fathom, but he had, and that was all that counted. We were in.

The windowless room was bathed in a red night-light, and despite Jacques's assertion that no autopsies took place here, there was an autopsy table in the middle of the room, its shiny metal surface so clinical and forbidding in that room of death. Jacques swore under his breath and then said, "Wait here. I forgot something. Back in five."

I felt a moment of panic as he turned abruptly and headed back to the door we came through.

"Where are you going?"

But either he didn't hear me or he didn't want to, because all I heard was the quiet click of the door as it shut behind him. I shivered. I was in the morgue all alone. The room was windowless and the eerie red light, the colour of blood, made me feel like death was a living breathing thing out to get me. The room was bathed in it. Even the air seemed strangled, suffocating, inert. And the faint hissing sound coming from a grate in the wall was the voice of the dead trying to smother me. I shook myself, trying to dislodge images that were careering at me like a movie whose director had lost control. I was here for a reason. I had to ground myself.

I surveyed the room. Metal chests of drawers lined one wall, the contents of which I could imagine were instruments of death, but I didn't want to go there, had to stop my mind from its wild ride.

And then I saw them.

Two square metal doors one above the other, with a single lever handle on each one. They looked so innocuous, so anticlimactic, as to be the storage places for human bodies. But there was no mistaking what they were. Even though I had never seen one in real life, I had seen these stainless-steel refrigerated units on TV countless times.

I crept over to them, sidling up to them as if afraid they'd bite me. They were so shiny and clean. It seemed impossible that something dead could be inside them. I reached for the bottom door and opened it. The unit had a gigantic tray inside it, which you could pull out to view what was on it. This one was empty. I opened the top one and closed my eyes and held my breath. Slowly I opened one eye and drew in my breath.

Very definitely Mavis. Very definitely dead.

The scarf was gone, but a tiny silver cross was still around her neck, and what life there once had been was gone.

I suppose if I had been religious I would have crossed myself or something, but all I felt was sadness. And that was when I heard voices coming down the corridor. I looked wildly around for a place to hide. There was a locked closet and nothing else.

I nearly gagged when I realized the only place to hide was in the bottom drawer. I opened the door and got down on my hands and knees and looked inside. So cold and dark and claustrophobic. Supporting myself on my elbows, I squirmed in backward and pulled on the edge of the door, almost but not quite closing it.

I let out an involuntary gasp as the cold steel touched my body and the darkness was almost absolute, except for a tiny crack in the door. I'm not claustrophobic, but the walls were so close upon me, the air so smothering, and the cold so penetrating and indifferent that I felt the welling up of panic and envisioned the walls slowly moving in and squeezing my body until the life was flattened right out of me.

It was visceral and it was real, but so were the voices in my head yelling at me to get the hell out. A very reasonable order. Except for the other voices, which were now coming through the door. Was this really happening to me? I pulled my hand up to my face and bit it. Definitely real. Definitely happening to me. And then the voices were in the room.

I had my hand on the door, lightly gripping it by its interior edge. I tried looking out the crack, but whoever they were, they were not in my line of vision and I could only hear them intermittently. The closest one to me was a woman. Of that I was sure. The other had a low voice I could not hear very well, so I couldn't tell if it was a man with a high voice or a woman with a low voice.

"She saw her …

"… have to do something.

"… she's talking.

"… knows too much.

"… police snooping.

"Leave it with me … I'll think of something."

And suddenly the speaker I could hear moved closer to me and I shrank back, if that was humanly possible in the small space I was in. There was only one person she or he could have been talking about, and that was me.

Well, there was a bright side. At least I wasn't psycho. Mavis had died. I didn't know how and I didn't know why. What I did know was that I needed to find out, because if Mavis hadn't committed suicide, then whoever had killed her might kill me. In my sleep. Just like Mavis. The words I had just overheard were ominous and I felt a chill of fear in my gut. Had I just heard my own death sentence?

I was getting very cold. My legs and arms were numb and I had a sudden cramp in my leg that had me doing a silent scream to ease the pain. Nothing like getting a charley horse while trapped inside a morgue fridge.

"What's this door doing open?"

The voice, a woman's, was right there by my ear, and I jumped and then my heart leaped as I saw her hand, minus one finger, push the door closed with a resounding thud. I pulled my own hand back just in time. I lay there shivering in my cold dark tomb, wondering if I should pound on the door and take the chance that I might escape my probable murderers, once they released me from the fridge, or wait and hope Jacques would find me.

I lay there listening to myself breathing. I could hear my heart beating in my ears and feel it thumping in my chest and I felt suffocated. After a few minutes I couldn't stand it any longer and that was when I realized the material from the right sleeve of my shirt was caught in the door. I struggled to pull it free but it wouldn't budge.

And then I really panicked. I was getting colder by the second and having trouble breathing, and I saw myself gasping out the rest of my life in a glorified fridge. I yelled. I rapped the door with my left hand and I did it over and over until I was exhausted.

And then the door opened. I didn't know whether I was about to be murdered, having just been rescued from certain death, or whether it would be my salvation.

It was the latter. Jacques.

"Nice-colour shirt," he said as he pulled my frigid body out of the tray by my shoulders. I looked down at my canary-yellow shirt.

"I might not have noticed it sticking out if it had been some dull colour."

I didn't say anything, I was so cold. My teeth were jumping around and hitting each other like castanets. Jacques was still holding me by my shoulders and I wasn't sure if the chill down my spine was because I was practically hypothermic or because Jacques was holding me. I looked up at him and he suddenly drew me to him, enveloping me in his arms and holding me so tightly that I could hardly breathe. Definitely not all hypothermic, because hypothermia does not usually come with a frisson of excitement. He was rubbing me vigorously with his hands and I didn't want it to end. I could have stood there in his arms forever and been happy, but we weren't exactly in a safe place and so the hug ended and we were back in the morgue. The owners of the two voices, one mysterious and the other not so much, had left the lights on and the room suddenly looked ordinary, clinical but ordinary. Jacques must have just missed them.

He picked up a camera from the floor where he must have dropped it to rescue me and said, "Had to go back for my camera. Did you find her? We need photographs."

I nodded and pointed to the top drawer. As he approached it, we heard a voice call out somewhere in the corridor, so Jacques moved with lightning speed to the closet door I'd tried earlier.

"It's locked," I said.

He pulled his picks from his pocket and fumbled with the door as I stood, like a deer caught in headlights, waiting for the morgue door to open. But Jacques was first and we tumbled through the door, mere seconds before we heard people moving about in the morgue and talking. We were in a supply closet that was only slightly less claustrophobic than the fridge had been. I was slowly starting to warm up, but my chattering teeth sounded so loud that I had to consciously keep my mouth open to keep my teeth from hitting against one another. We stayed huddled in that little closet for a long time after the noises had stopped coming from the morgue. Jacques held me tightly in his arms, trying to warm me, the heat from his body slowly seeping into mine. I could hear his heart beating and feel his breath ruffling my hair. I almost forgot that we were in a rather precarious situation until Jacques finally released me. He opened the door cautiously and we were greeted with the same reddish light that had so disturbed me.

"Let's be quick," he said and he walked over and pulled out the top morgue drawer. As I joined him and looked inside, I suddenly felt disoriented and light-headed.

Mavis was gone.

chapter seven

I was thinking about my brother and my poor little niece and trying to warm up from the refrigerated morgue drawer when I looked out the seventh-floor window of my room and remembered it was winter. Now I vaguely recalled that Ryan had brought me my winter boots and coat on one of his recent visits, but nothing had registered — with the exception of the look of desperation in his eyes when he'd asked me how I was doing. He'd needed me to say I was okay and I couldn't. He'd been worried sick about Annie and worried sick about me, and I wasn't able to give him anything.

I focused on the streets below. They were where I used to roam as an undergraduate at the University of Toronto, and were now covered in a thick blanket of snow. The city was in the midst of a snowstorm, and the unwise, the unwary, or the unfortunate few who were out in this weather were embracing themselves, holding on to their coats against the cold north wind.

Out of the corner of my eye I saw movement, not down on the streets, but at my level. Something small and black. I peered through the swirling snow and felt a cold tendril of fear spiral inside me. It was a squirrel. A black squirrel. Part of me wondered how the hell a squirrel could be seven floors up a sheer wall in a raging snowstorm in the dead of winter. It must have come from the roof, I thought, even as another part of me thought I must be hallucinating. I watched its tiny feet gripping the cement as its inched downward headfirst and out of sight. But not before I heard someone exclaim, "Look at that! A squirrel!"

I was never happier to hear a real voice say those words and I turned to see Ella standing wide-eyed as she looked out the window beside me. She seemed so … human in her unguarded moment. But then the sentiment vanished and the nurse in her returned, holding my evening pills in her little white cup. *Why is she bringing me my pills?* I wondered. *What's wrong with me going to the dispensary?*

"Thought I'd bring you these myself because I wanted to talk to you about how you're doing."

I looked at her suspiciously. Someone might be trying to kill me and one of them was a woman missing a finger. It stretched the bounds of coincidence to think there could be two people missing fingers in this hospital. So simple to take me down with a drug overdose and a cringing "Mea culpa, I'm so sorry. It was an accident."

I eyed the pills, suddenly trying hard not to look suspicious. She could just as easily whip out a syringe and jab me with some lethal untraceable concoction. She gave me the little paper cup, and then she waited until I had tipped the contents into my mouth, before handing me a second cup of water. I turned slightly away from her, but not enough to arouse her suspicion and was doing acrobatics with my tongue, juggling the pills and sweeping them into my cheek. I looked at her out of the corner of my eye and our gazes locked. There was no menace in hers that I could see. Nothing to indicate she wanted to get rid of me. Had the hand really been missing a finger? Had it really been Ella? Could I trust my own mind?

But Ella had seen the squirrel, so my mind was functioning properly. I wondered then about calling the police, but what would I say and why would they believe a psych patient? It was my word against hers.

"Cordi, we need to talk about Mavis."

She took the cups from my hand and went and threw them in the wastebasket by the door. While her back was turned I spat out the pills and stuffed them under my pillow. She grabbed the one visitor's chair we had in the room and pulled it up near my bed. She gestured for me to sit on the mattress.

"What about her?"

"You seem to have it in your head that she died."

"She did die. And you saw her."

There was a fleeting look of frustration, or it could have been fear, on her face before she composed herself and said, "Sometimes people can misinterpret what they see."

"I misinterpreted?"

"Yes, you did," she said a little too eagerly. "Mavis just got very sick and had to be moved."

"But you know otherwise, don't you," I said flatly and she stared at me, unblinking.

"I will arrange for you to see Dr. Osborn again," she said. Then she got up and left me sitting there, but not without a backward glance in my direction, a glance that looked like a warning. I was still trying to interpret Ella's glance when Lucy galloped into the room, flinging blonde hair out of her sapphire eyes.

"I've got this great plan!" she said. "It's going to work, too. I'm going to be a stunt woman and be the double for all the famous actors." She blathered on about her idea, words running into words, flowing fast and furious, but when I held up my hand she stopped in mid-sentence and cocked her head at me.

"How well did you know Mavis?" I asked.

"You mean do, don't you? *Do* know her."

I nodded, making a mental note to talk about Mavis in the present tense.

"She's okay. Schizophrenic. Had some weird hallucinations. Strange family."

I raised my eyebrows.

"Her family is the Church of Scientology," Lucy explained. "Enough said."

"You mean she's a Scientologist?"

"Yeah, pretty much said that, didn't I?"

"What about her real family?"

"Mavis doesn't have a family. She's an orphan, and a very rich one."

"What happened to her family?"

"She killed them."

My face obviously looked the way I felt — stunned — because Lucy said, "No, really. She killed them. She was at the wheel of the family car with her father beside her and her mother in the back seat. The car blew a tire and she lost control. They flipped a bunch of times and landed upside down in a ditch full of water. Mavis got out but her parents drowned."

"Jesus," I said. "Poor Mavis."

"Not really," said Lucy. "She inherited everything from her parents. Set her up for many lifetimes."

The conversation had tired me out and I lay down on my bed and fell asleep. They say dreams can help you sort out the nightmares of life, but my dreams were just nightmares. I did not awake refreshed or rejuvenated. My mind was a fog of ideas merging with my dreams. One thing I was sure of: Mavis was dead and there was nobody looking for the reason. Human nature says you take the path of least resistance and if it had been accidental or a suicide, alerting the authorities would have been the easiest step. But they hadn't taken that route, whoever *they* were. She'd been spirited away and we'd all been told that she was alive and recuperating elsewhere in the hospital. Was that to make us feel better? It seemed like a rather elaborate thing to do. But I knew what I saw.

I wandered down the hall to the cafeteria and the common room. There were two large lumpy sofas and a couple of recliners forming a semicircle around the TV, where I had sat with Austin. There were a couple of chairs along the bank of south-facing windows — they were for the antisocial among us or for those who didn't want to watch TV.

No one was watching TV when I arrived. No one was there at all and I picked up a magazine and sat down on the sofa to read. I should have known that was a bad idea for someone who was feeling rather antisocial, because someone was bound to come in and corner me. But the person who cornered me wasn't who I expected.

"Hi, Cordi." I looked up from my magazine and saw my brother, Ryan. Even in winter he looked like summer, his face littered with freckles and his hair the colour of honey, tinged with red. He searched my face, looking for a clue to my mood. I smiled and the anxious look on his face evaporated. He plunked himself down beside me and we sat in silence for a while.

We had often sat in silence and it usually enveloped us like a warm and friendly glove, but this time it seemed sterile, as though that was all there was between us — silence and nothing more. I shivered. So we talked about the farm for a few minutes and the hired hands who were running it for us, and then we talked about Annie and her constant medical appointments and treatment. And then we came to an impasse. Ryan began rummaging in his pockets as if to break the silence with motion, and I looked at him with pity. He wanted so badly for me to be well. It didn't matter that I was well, or close to it. To relieve his anxiety, he had to *believe* it.

"So what's the doc say? Everybody wants you out of here," he said a little too brightly.

I smiled and almost told him about Mavis's death, but some survival instinct stopped me. I was afraid he wouldn't believe me, that he would think it was all a figment of my imagination, especially when I told him the hospital staff denied it. And it would worry him. So I said nothing about Mavis and the morgue and the ominous conversation I had overheard.

"What are you looking for?" I finally asked him as he continued his search. I was aware that he was making a bit of a show of it and really wanted me to ask him what he was looking for. But he didn't answer. Instead, he stood up and began going through all his myriad pockets. He'd always been like that. He was the kind of man who, as a little boy, carried bits of string, pebbles, rocks, a pocketknife, and any other little treasure until his pockets were bulging and he had to empty them all to find what he wanted. He didn't quite have to do that now, but he did pull some credit-card slips and some folded sheets of paper out of his pockets before he found what he was looking for. He held it up for me to see, a big grin on his face.

I squinted at the two pieces of crumpled cardboard in his hand. He fanned them out. Two tickets to something. I reached out for them, but he pulled back on me. He had always done that, too, but this time it was as though he was acting his part, trying too hard. I pushed a smile onto my face and gestured with my hand. His grin got bigger and he finally handed the tickets to me.

"Today's afternoon's game," he said. "Leafs versus Montreal."

I didn't say anything.

"If we leave in ten minutes, we can walk," he said somewhat uncertainly. "You love to walk. It's a real winter day out there, but that's never stopped us before. And if we walk we don't have to deal with the subway or the parking. Besides, I forgot my cellphone so we can't use the rover parking app."

I looked up at him, then back down at the tickets. They must have cost him a fortune.

"But I can't just leave," I said.

"Why not? You know you're not committed. Besides, Dr. Osborn thinks it would be a good idea for your first outing to be with me."

I digested that information rather slowly and he began to get alarmed.

"Don't you want to come?"

I pulled myself together and said, "Yes, of course I do." But I wasn't sure what a vast crowd of people might do to me in my state of mind.

Ryan grabbed my hand and pulled me up off the sofa as if we were kids again, and there was nothing for it but to go and get my coat and boots. When we opened the front door of the hospital, winter was waiting. My body was assaulted by the huge change in temperature. *How vulnerable we are,* I thought. Just one universal power outage shy of freezing to death. It *was* a beautiful day now, and we eventually ended up going east on Dundas to University and then all the way down University.

We got as far Richmond Street before I finally blurted out my story about Mavis. I watched his face as best I could while we walked: confusion, love, pity, indecision, even fear. But not belief, at least not that I could see.

"How do you know for sure she's dead?" he asked.

"Because she isn't alive?"

Ryan grimaced and shoved his hands into his pockets. Despite the sun, there was a biting wind.

"And you think the authorities are hiding it so you guys won't get scared." It wasn't a question, but I nodded anyway. We were standing at a red light at King Street and I started stamping my feet, which were getting numb.

Ryan put his hands on my shoulders and said, "You say this Jacques guy was with you in the morgue?"

I nodded.

"And he saw Mavis too?"

I knew where he was going and I had forgotten, perhaps on purpose, to tell him that Jacques had not seen Mavis.

"No," I said, and he searched my face for I know not what. The light finally turned green and we walked in silence to Front Street, but this time the silence was noisy and rife with unspoken thoughts.

We began mingling with the crowds at Front Street and moved in a stream into Union Station, its vast high ceiling and enormous arched multi-paned window at one end making it feel like a cathedral. I felt like an ant among many, following a scent to the prize. And yet, it was strangely comforting to be so anonymous.

We finally found our way into the Air Canada Centre and our seats high up at one end, two people among some eighteen thousand. *How many*, I wondered, *were playing hooky from school or work?* But then I remembered it was Sunday.

We all stood for the national anthem. The singer, dwarfed by the expanse of gleaming ice and the tiers of unending seats, looked too small to be the source of the booming voice that came from the loudspeakers. Then we all sat back down, the puck was dropped, and the game started. Despite the old Habs-Leafs rivalry, both teams were playing as if they hadn't slept for a week and I began to watch the crowds. Every colour of the rainbow was represented in the clothing people wore, like a haphazard mosaic or a patchwork quilt. Many people were talking animatedly with each other and some were yelling at the players.

And that was when I saw him.

He was sitting ten seats to my left and three rows down. Shock of white hair. Early forties, handsome. Osborn. What were the odds?

He was sitting beside one of the young patients from my floor. My opinion of him went way up. I thought it was awfully nice of the doctor to take a patient to a hockey game. I watched him for a while, and when a fight broke out on the ice, I was happy to see him glower and grip his companion's shoulder.

I turned my attention back to the game and watched two grown men, gloves off, punching each other to try to get revenge for some wrong, perceived or real. The fans booed and cheered. Whatever happened to sportsmanship? If all the world conducted its business, solved its problems the way hockey players do, we'd be living in a bloodbath.

At last, the fight broken up by the refs, the game resumed. And when one player made a breakaway, outsmarted the goalie, and scored, all was forgiven. The fans roared, almost as much as they did during the fight. Cripes, even hockey was getting me down. But at least it was all real, the sights, the smells, Ryan beside me. All real. All mine.

We took a taxi back to the hospital because I was so cold. The sun had set and it was snowing by the time we reached the hospital. Ryan didn't walk up with me, which I took as a good sign. I didn't feel like going to my room and there was no one in the common room, so I went back to the same sofa and found the same magazine.

"Warmed up yet?" I looked up to see Jacques hovering above me, his blond hair swept loosely back off his forehead. He was gripping a toothpick between his teeth. I wondered again if he was a smoker. Did he chaw down on his cigarettes as hard as he did the toothpick? And was the surrogate working for him?

I smiled up at him. "No. Still chilled." I wondered what he was thinking. We had shared a strange moment together. And had his hug been more than just him trying to warm me up? I was very aware that he had never actually seen Mavis's body and we had no photo to prove she was dead. Did he still believe me?

As if he was reading my thoughts he said, "Too bad I didn't get the photo." Noncommittal.

"Yeah," I said intelligently.

"But you said you saw her on the slab."

"Yeah," I said again, wondering where this was going.

"I believe you," he said. Just like that. I was taken aback and as I studied his impenetrable face, my neck spasmed from all that looking up and I grabbed it with one hand to rub it.

"Did you hear me?" he said.

"Yes," I said. "Why?"

"Why what?"

"Why do you believe me?"

He looked a bit nonplussed as he sucked in some air and stroked his chin, the kind of chin that needed shaving twice a day. His hair had fallen over his eyes and he swept it back again with one hand as I thought about him being an alcoholic smoker. An addictive personality.

That could mean any number of problems. Dangerous footing. Yet he seemed so in control.

"I think you're not as sick as they say you are. That you are quite capable of telling the difference between a dead body and a living one. That someone is messing with you." He hesitated, as if he had something more to say, but then thought better of it. I had the impression that he was hiding something from me. I really didn't want to just ask him, so I tried a new tack.

"She has no family," I said. "No one to look into her death. If they've covered it up, no one will ever know."

"That's why we have to do something."

It was sweet to hear the "we." I didn't feel so alone.

"Okay, so what do we know so far?" I asked.

Jacques sat down beside me and my heart did a little twirligig as his leg pressed against mine. To distract myself from his presence — and it *was* a presence — I answered my own question. "Mavis died and there was a scarf wound around her neck."

"We know the nurses would never have let her have a scarf, so where did it come from? Who smuggled it in?" asked Jacques.

I shrugged as he shifted his weight closer to me, and the shrug turned into a shiver.

"So it could be the murder weapon," he said. It felt creepy to hear those words in all their starkness, and I pictured Mavis dead on the bed, the scarf wrapped around her.

"Yeah," I said. "Someone could have strangled her with the scarf."

"Or *she* could have," said Jacques. I gave him a look and he threw his hands up in the air.

"All right. All right. Hard to do that. We've been there before."

"So, murder it is?" I said.

"Murder it might be." And then he reached over with his right hand and squeezed my knee.

I left Jacques and went back to my room. Mavis's death had not resulted in our being evicted from our room, for which I had mixed feelings. All sorts of questions were storming my brain, and not all of them were about Mavis. Jacques was becoming a serious distraction and I didn't know if that was good or bad. It had been well over a year since Patrick and I had gone our separate ways and I wasn't really looking for a new relationship. Especially not when I'd been hospitalized with a mental health issue and so had Jacques.

No one was in my room. I put my coat and boots away in the closet and sat down on my bed and stared at Mavis's bed. Now empty. All that was left of her life was a bed made up neatly with hospital corners and a thin beige velour blanket. So ordinary. Just an empty bed. Had she known she was going to die?

I looked out the window, hoping to see the squirrel, but all I saw was a swirl of snowflakes beating themselves against the glass. The sun had set, but the snow still glittered in the ambient light of the city. Suddenly I felt a need to be outside again, in the cold early-evening air, but on my own, with no one looking after me. I pulled on my coat and boots and left with such a sense of urgency that it wasn't until I reached the front entrance that I realized I'd forgotten my wallet. I'd also forgotten to sign myself out.

I skittered back to my room to find a member of the cleaning staff hovering over my bed. She turned and looked guiltier than the cat with canary feathers protruding from its mouth. She flapped her hands and backed off. She was tiny. Even I could have handled her with one hand.

"What are you doing?" I asked, glancing about to make sure there was no one else with her. She hesitated and glanced out the window as if looking for help.

"I was taking out the garbage." I looked at where she stood, a good ten feet away from the garbage bag she'd propped against the wastebasket. *Jesus.* Was she after me? Did that mean that Ella had recruited someone to get me? That I had to be worried about everyone and not just Ella?

The woman was wringing her hands, clearly anxious. "I saw a squirrel. I went to see and rubbed my eyes. How could a squirrel be there?" She gave me an uncertain smile, then retrieved the garbage bag, and hurried out of the room.

Plausible story if the premise was correct. And I knew it was correct because I had seen the squirrel. Therefore her story was logical. She wasn't after me.

I hadn't thought about where I wanted to go, just that I wanted to be outside and moving. Even a big city can be brought to its knees by weather, and the snow had crippled the sidewalks and roads. People and cars were moving at less than half speed and all the noises of the city were muffled by the snow, so that it almost felt like being in a forest, where the trees were buildings and the streets were frozen rivers. *How fast weather can change the city,* I thought. I walked and I walked. One stretch of sidewalk that I came upon had only one set of footprints.

A man with a long stride. I followed in his steps almost doing the splits at each stride, the snow well above the ankles of my boots.

At times like this people band together to help a car stuck in the snow or an elderly man trying to cross the road. But it is also solitary. You're an island unto yourself, separated from the world by the swirling snow that blurs the vision and dulls the senses of touch and hearing, all swaddled up in clothes, safe from the elements. As long as you have a warm place to go back to. I had passed several homeless people curled up in shop doorways or lying in sleeping bags on grates where the warm air would thaw them. I went into some of the funky stores on Markham Street and ventured into the giant emporium that was Honest Ed's.

Bigger than a giant hangar and more convoluted and frustrating than a maze, it spanned numerous floors and half floors, blind alleys, and open-ended rooms that went on forever. It was full of people and endless bins of endless merchandise you don't even know you want until you see it. I suddenly felt empty, watching all these people looking so busy and occupied, and me just biding time, waiting to get better. I didn't buy a thing. I just walked down aisle after aisle. It was not that I didn't see anything I wanted. I did. But I had no energy to find the checkout and stand in line. I left the store ten minutes after I wanted to because I couldn't find an exit, which gave me a panicky feeling. I felt truly sorry for Leo because I knew my panic was magnitudes weaker than his.

The snow was coming down in a desultory fashion now and I walked through it thinking about Mavis and missing fingers and how it was a good thing that I didn't

want to die. It meant I was getting better. It was the cold
that finally brought me back out of myself and I had to
search out street signs to figure out where I was. I was
tired and I had walked a long way from the hospital, but
when I looked at my watch only an hour had gone by. I
spotted a subway entrance and so I took it.

It was evening and there were quite a few people on
the platform. It was one of those split platforms where
the trains are separated from each other by the platform
itself. It was cold and drafty and dirty and the tiled
floors were covered in slush from the snow falling off
hundreds of winter boots. I stood on the yellow danger
line halfway down the platform and looked to the left
from where the train would come, the tunnel dark and
empty. I looked in the other direction. Two dark and
empty tunnels. And then lights, growing bigger, piercing
the gloom of the tunnel on my left, bringing lightness
out of the dark. I shivered involuntarily at the imag-
ery, when I should have been paying attention to what
was happening around me. Without warning, someone
plunged into me.

I lost my balance and pitched forward, the gleaming metal of the tracks burning their twin images into
my brain. Thoughts and feelings are so much faster
than words. I felt sick, scared, thought, *This can't be
happening to me, I'm going to die,* all in the space of
the two seconds it took me to fall onto the tracks. I
was pitching forward, so I let myself go, hitting the
surface between the two tracks with my upper back
and shoulder and then rolling to break the fall. I came
up standing, facing the fast-approaching train with its
mesmerizing twin beams.

I was aware of people yelling and waving their arms, trying to get the train to stop. I was aware, too, that there was nowhere for me to duck out of the way. The far side of the track was a sheer wall right beside the rail and there was no lip under the platform to protect me. So I turned and ran. As fast as it was possible to run. I could hear the brakes of the train screeching behind me, knew it was coming at me, knew I could not waste time to turn and look, knew that I also wanted to *see* the death that was facing me. I overcame that urge and kept running down the uneven track toward the darkness of the tunnel.

It seemed ironic that a dark tunnel would mean my salvation when it's the phrase "light at the end of the tunnel" that people use to describe getting out of trouble and getting out of depression. I ran, in my clunky winter boots, my coat flapping, the train at my back. I felt like a hiker who has seen a bear between herself and safety, and turns to run, waiting on every stride for the ripping sound of the bear's claws in her flesh.

And then I felt it, the slight grazing on the backs of my legs, a mere caress, as I was ten feet from the tunnel. I pitched forward and grabbed my head with my hands in a ridiculous attempt to protect it. But when nothing happened to me, no tearing of flesh, no rending of limbs, I took my hands from my head and looked up. The train had run out of steam.

"She's okay!" someone yelled.

I felt a pair of strong arms help me up and I let their owner lead me down the tunnel to the steps and up to the very end of the platform. I was feeling hot and shaky and I just wanted to sit down. So I did. Right at the end of the platform. People milled about me and I could hear snippets of conversation.

"I saw her fall."

"She went over like a sack of potatoes."

"She must have tripped."

"No, no, surely she fainted."

And then a voice, alone among the babble, said, "She was pushed."

chapter eight

I insisted I didn't need to go to the ER. There was absolutely nothing wrong with me and the paramedics who arrived on the scene said I was good to go. The police suggested I call a friend but I said no, that I was okay. When they found out where I lived they insisted on driving me home. They said they were heading in that direction anyway. So I let them. What else could I do? I couldn't have them drop me off at the hospital. If they thought I was not right in the head, it would colour everything I had said to them. They wouldn't believe me. There was so much prejudice surrounding mental illness. Then again, there was no doubt I had fallen onto the tracks and there were lots of people to corroborate that. Maybe I was just being paranoid.

At least I hadn't told them that I thought someone was trying to kill me. Why hadn't I? Did I doubt myself that much, or was it because whoever had said I was pushed had disappeared into the crowd and nobody else had seen anything? The police waited politely in the circular drive of Governor's Manor condominium townhomes, where Ryan had rented me a furnished place from a friend, until I had let myself in. I waved and they pulled away.

The apartment was in darkness. My timer for the lights must have been broken. There was mail strewn all over the floor and still more piled up on my hall table. Ryan must have come in and done that.

She was pushed.

The words came storming out at me from the darkness of my home away from home, and I stood there momentarily paralyzed by my thoughts. Had someone just tried to kill me? Could it have been Ella? Had she been following me? What time was her shift over?

I felt so alone, standing there in the hall and feeling sorry for myself. I really missed my little log cabin on our farm in the shadow of the Eardley Escarpment. I mentally doused my mind with cold water and turned on the lights. Everything was as I had left it on that night that Ryan had come and brought me to his home, scared and very depressed. I wandered around the apartment, picking up my belongings, a little statue of a whale, a book, my mail. I wanted to stay, but I knew I couldn't. I had a 9:00 p.m. curfew and it was 8:30.

The cabbie dropped me off at the hospital at 8:55. The snow had stopped falling now, and I walked down a newly shovelled, winding path to the side door, which was the entrance to a small two-storey cinder-block building that had been added on like a limpet to a rock. This was the smokers' haunt and even in this weather there were four people huddled by the door, playing Russian roulette with curfew. There were giant icicles hanging from the roof above the door and I stepped quickly across the threshold. Jacques was there, amongst the smokers, shoulders hunched, an unlit cigarette dangling from his hand. I hesitated, not knowing what to do and then he smiled. I smiled back and our eyes met.

Can eyes kiss? It sure felt like it. He opened the door for me.

"I seem to always be trying to get you warm," he said as his arms encircled me from behind and stopped me dead in my tracks, physically as well as emotionally. He gave me a breathtaking hug then, and let me go. I was trying to find something clever to say as he went ahead of me and pushed the up button on the elevator.

"You all right?" he asked, a worried look on his face. *Do I look that bad?* I wondered. I wanted to tell him right then and there about my fall onto the subway tracks, but we were late and there was no time. We had to return to our rooms.

I had missed dinner and my stomach was churning, as much from the lack of food as the trauma I'd undergone. Such a sharp contrast to my apartment, the cold walls of my room, the bare linoleum floor, the metal beds, with all four solid sides flush to the floor, their meagre blankets, and the metal bedside tables with a single drawer and a little cabinet underneath. Bigger than a jail cell, but almost as sterile.

Kit was sitting on her bed when I entered our room, her red curls springing as usual to every point on the compass. She had laid out a large hardcover picture book on her bed and on it she was meticulously sorting a box of Smarties, the blues, the browns, the oranges, the yellows, the greens, all laid out in neat square patterns with the red ones set to one side and forming a circle.

"Do you like the red ones best?" I asked, trying not to drool over the candy.

"They have to be eaten in a certain way or they don't taste the same and you'll get sick," she said. She didn't look up.

"Red ones last?" I asked, thinking I knew what she was going to say. Save the best for last. And it suited her red hair.

She looked up then, a flash of impatience creasing her face.

"I don't eat the crimson ones anymore," she said.

I waited.

"They're bad luck."

I waited some more.

"They're the colour of blood," and she shivered and pushed the red ones, one by agonizing one back into the Smarties box, got up and placed them in the wastebasket. She returned to the bed and ate a single green Smartie before looking up at me.

"There wasn't any blood, was there." Kit said this as more a statement of fact than a question, and it was disconcerting.

I didn't know what to say. Was she talking about Mavis? Did that mean she believed me?

I shook my head. It seemed safer than saying anything.

"Was she really dead?"

I chose my words carefully. "The staff say no."

"What do *you* say?" She ate another green smartie. My stomach whined like a begging dog.

"I thought she was dead, but I guess I was mistaken." For some reason I felt the need to lie about Mavis. Maybe I didn't want to upset Kit. But that made me complicit with the cover-up. She ate the last green smartie and moved on to the yellow ones, one at a time, her trip around the circumference of the book, a clockwise journey. That meant the brown ones would be last. I'd never known anyone to like the brown smarties best. Save the worst 'til last?

"You need to trust yourself more," Kit said with her head down, but it was the way she said it, as much as what she said, that made me pause. It was almost as though she knew something, but was afraid to say.

I was about to do a little probing when the night nurse came in to tell us it was lights out in half an hour. I sat down on my bed and watched Kit eating her smarties.

"How long have you known Mavis?" I asked, not sure what I was trying to jumpstart.

"She was here when I came."

"Did you like her?"

"What was not to like about her? She was kind."

"Can you think of any reason why someone would want her dead?" To hell with lies.

"You mean, if she is dead." Kit locked eyes with me, and again I had that disconcerting feeling that she was hiding something. She looked away.

"Okay," said Kit. "Mavis was really messy. There were days when I wanted to strangle her."

Strangle. Odd choice of word, I thought.

"Other than that," Kit went on, "I can't think of any motive for anyone. People liked her."

Lucy interrupted us at that point as she bounded into the room. She and Kit exchanged glances and Kit's face became an inscrutable mask as she turned away. Lucy stared at her, her own face looking almost exasperated, as if Kit had done something wrong. It was a strange little tableau but it passed, as Lucy, apparently needing to talk, described the whole story of a TV show she had just seen. I couldn't help but notice that she was talking only to me. Not once did she look at Kit after that initial exchange of glances, yet I was pretty sure they had been friendly before. Figuring out what was going on between them was a job beyond my pay scale.

After lights out I lay in bed, nursing my grumbling stomach and listening as the silence gave way to the even breathing of my two sleeping roommates. Quietly I got up and retrieved the Smarties box from the wastebasket. By the light of the moon streaming in my window I ate all nine of those ruby red Smarties, the colour of blood, and to hell with superstition.

Normally I like to sleep in but I woke at 6:00 a.m. and I couldn't get back to sleep. I was reluctantly getting into the routine of the floor. We were woken up at 8:00 a.m. — which was way too early for me — for 8:15 breakfast. After that we had time to ourselves until classes started at 9:00. It was unspoken but understood that if you didn't go to at least some of them, you weren't getting better. Lunch was at noon and classes started again at 1:00 and ran to 4:00. None of the classes were more than an hour long and they ran the gamut from self-help stuff and self-confidence boosters to spiritual classes and cognitive behavioural therapy, plus crafts like drawing and painting. Dinner was at 5:00 and then we had a long stretch until snack time at 8:00 and lights out at 10:00.

I got to breakfast bang on 8:15, just as the cook was raising the metal accordion window that hid the kitchen from view. I was so hungry that I went back for what seconds there were. Usually we were allowed more toast, but everything else was off the menu once we'd had a first helping. Today, however, was different. The cook, incredibly, had made too much bacon and a couple of others and I got seconds.

I sat by myself and surveyed people as they ate. Most of them were still in pajamas and I wondered what their lives were like at home. They suddenly all seemed so lonely and injured and pathetic. I waited around for a while, hoping Jacques would show, but he must have had an early doctor's appointment or something.

As I was heading back down the hall to my room someone called my name. I turned to see Ella walking toward me. She was wearing a utilitarian pants uniform, all white, that failed to hide the voluptuous figure underneath. I hated having to admit something good about her when her intentions toward me might be anything but. I stopped and waited for her to catch up to me, wondering all the while what dire plans she had for me and if I'd be able to outsmart her, as I had, barely, on the subway — if indeed she was the one who'd pushed me. I couldn't be certain, of course, but it made me more determined to find out what had happened to Mavis.

"Dr. Osborn will see you at 9:30." Ella didn't seem like a murderer. She was calm and looked me in the eye, as if everything was perfectly normal. I thanked her and watched as she walked past me to the nursing station. I went into my room, where I lay down on my bed and tried to read a book until my appointment with Dr. Osborn. At 9:25 Ella came and got me. We walked through the empty cafeteria to the door that Mavis had gone through for the last time, and I watched as Ella unlocked it and let me through. She didn't stay with me this time. I knew how to get to the doctor's office. Osborn's door was slightly ajar and I knocked lightly on it. There was the rushing sound of a babbling brook and then his voice.

"Come in," he said. He was sitting at his wooden desk, but he stood up when I came in and walked around and gestured toward the sofa, where I'd sat last time. But instead, I chose the chair and he took the sofa, without blinking an eye. I wondered how many of his patients always sat in the same place, visit after visit. What was it like to listen to people's despair day after day after day? Did it become like an assembly line? Or was it more like a never-ending puzzle, with Osborn tweaking medications, hoping to find the right cocktail of drugs to ease the pain?

"How are you?" he said. I thought about that phrase, how it is often used as an icebreaker, like talking about the weather.

But I knew he really meant the question, and so I said, "Okay, I guess."

"Just okay?"

"I don't know. I'm feeling a little shaky."

"Why do you say that?"

"I found my roommate dead in her bed."

"The nurses told me about that," he said. We stared unblinking at each other. He was part of the cover-up. Would he tell me the truth?

"Tell me about what you thought you saw." So I did.

After I had finished he looked at me thoughtfully and said, "I'm beginning to think that depression isn't your only problem. You might be suffering from some sort of paranoia, as well." He started to tell me more, but I wasn't listening. I was too anxious about Mavis and I interrupted him.

"What's happened to Mavis?" I blurted out. The need to know was overwhelming. But his answer was underwhelming.

"Cordi, I'm sorry. You know I can't discuss other patients. I'm just concerned with getting your illness under control."

"She seemed so happy, you know?" I said. "When she came back from her electroshock treatment, she was so pleased that the nurse had got the stain out of her T-shirt. So happy."

I glanced up at Osborn just in time to see a strange look on his face, as if what I had said puzzled him, but then he cleared his throat and said, "I don't think you need another ECT just yet, but it's something we should keep in mind."

Another? I was nonplussed and horrified. "What do you mean, 'another'?" I asked, my voice barely a whisper.

And then the loud and strident ringing of the fire alarm intruded on my fear and confusion.

Osborn looked at me and said, "We'll finish this later. We need to evacuate." As if what he had said wasn't its own ten-alarm fire.

chapter nine

Usually a fire alarm in the dead of winter in a hospital is not just a fire drill, so everybody was told to move down the stairwell and stay calm. But we knew that we were seven flights up in a building presumably on fire and could get trapped, for all anyone knew, in that stuffy little stairwell. So the exhortation to remain calm wasn't all that effective. People were running down the stairs, some pushing past others. I was being jostled from all sides and at one point I stumbled and felt myself falling. I reached out wildly for anything to grab on to, and someone grabbed me, steadied me from behind. I looked around and saw that it was Dr. Osborn.

"Slowly, Cordi, slowly," he said.

Which royally pissed me off because I had been going more slowly than most, heeding the "be calm" directive. But then I felt uncharitable. He had, after all, just saved me from a fall.

I hadn't made it to the second floor when the PA system came on to say it had been a false alarm and we could return to our floors. The elevators at the second floor were jammed with people and I knew it would be the same on every floor, so I went back to the stairs and started climbing.

"You too, eh?" a voice said from behind me.

Gravelly. Deep. Exciting. *Jacques.*

I turned. "Didn't think a smoker could climb six flights," I said, and immediately regretted the words. I smiled at him to erase any sting.

"Maybe I can't. We're only on the second floor. Ask me when we get to the seventh."

I was very aware of his footsteps behind me as I started to climb, and was surprised at how light-footed he was for such a large man. When we got to the fourth floor I took pity on him and stopped to take a rest I didn't need. But he was right there with me, no laboured breathing, no sweaty forehead. I had stopped too soon on the landing and forced him to stop one step below me. Even with the added step he was still taller than I was and it made me feel all warm and fuzzy.

"Any further ahead on how Mavis died?" he asked.

I tried to remember where I had left off with him, what he knew and what he didn't.

"Are you having second thoughts?" he said, brushing his hand against my shoulder.

"About what?"

"About what happened."

"Dr. Osborn seems to think I should. Or rather, he insinuated."

Jacques raised his eyebrows. "Did he threaten you?"

"Why would you think that?"

"Just sayin'." Jacques had confused me. I wasn't sure what he meant and then I lost my train of thought. I stepped back and he stepped up onto the landing, making me crane my neck to see the green of his eyes.

"You know, I make a pretty good bodyguard. If anyone should threaten you."

I was quiet after he said that.

"Has someone threatened you?" Jacques continued.

"I don't know. Maybe."

"Maybe?"

So I told him about the subway.

"Jesus. You could have been killed."

"That might have been the intent, yes," I said wryly.

"Do you think you were pushed?"

"Someone barged into me. There's no question about that, but somebody could have just tripped and fallen against me. I was standing pretty close to the edge."

"But you said that someone said you were pushed."

"Yeah, I know. But I could have misheard and he actually said, 'Maybe she was pushed,' not 'she was pushed.'"

"What did the police say when you told them?"

"I didn't, because I wasn't sure." He looked at me in a way that made me feel stupid. And I guess I was. I should have told the police, but surely the security cameras would show what had happened. And maybe someone else had heard what I heard.

I looked at Jacques then and thought of Ella and her missing finger and her calm demeanor and her big, incredibly voluptuous body. He brushed his hand gently across my cheek and pushed a strand of hair out of my eyes. I felt weak in the knees.

"What is it? Do you know who it is?" he said. I couldn't exactly tell him the effect he was having on me by standing so close and caressing me, so I thought again about Ella and her finger. And then I thought about not telling Jacques, the way I had not told anyone, but I needed to talk and he was the only one who had said he believed me. And I believed he meant it.

"When I was in the morgue I saw the hand of one of the two people I overheard talking," I said in a rush.

Jacques inclined his head.

"It was missing a finger."

"Ella," said Jacques, and let out a long low whistle.

I told him then about what I'd heard her say — that I knew Mavis was dead, that I knew too much, and something had to be done. When I was finished he whistled again.

"Not much doubt that she was talking about you, eh?" he said. "But then you're easy to talk about." I must have looked startled because he laughed and pulled me to him. "Relax, that was a compliment." And then he kissed me, right there on the landing, and my world exploded.

I couldn't stop thinking about Jacques. Couldn't stop feeling his lips on mine, his hands running up and down my body. When we left the stairwell and I was back in my room I lay down on my bed and nursed the little piece of happiness that was growing inside me. There wasn't room for any other thoughts for a long long time, and then suddenly I remembered my meeting with Osborn. I got out my cellphone, checked the battery, and called Ryan, thankful that I was at least allowed to keep the phone in my room, if not the cord. Ryan answered on the first ring. I blurted out what I had to say.

"Dr. Osborn told me I may need to have another electroshock treatment, another ECT sometime. You know, the procedure where you get zapped into a seizure by electricity," I said, making sure he knew exactly what I was talking about.

I could hear Ryan breathing at the other end of the line. His silence was telling.

"What did he mean by another?" I asked, my voice insistent and cold.

He didn't answer me.

"Are you still there?" I asked.

"Yeah. Yeah, I'm still here."

"Ryan? Did I have an ECT?" I made no attempt to hide the panic in my voice.

"Yes."

"And you knew?"

"Yes."

I was too stunned to say anything.

"Cordi, you have to understand. You were so sick. Dr. Osborn said it would help you, because nothing else was. You were too sick to make the decision."

"So you made it for me."

"Yes."

I felt tremendously violated. That something had been done to me without my permission, without my knowledge. And I had no memory of it. I don't know which was worse. I was desperate to get off the phone, because I was afraid I might say something to Ryan that I would regret.

But he needed something from me, it seemed, and I heard him ask, "Do you still think that woman is dead, Cordi?" His voice was tentative, almost apologetic, definitely apprehensive, waiting for an answer that, either way, would not assuage his fears. A *yes* answer would chill him and a *no* answer would just have him asking, "Are you lying to make me feel better?" So I changed the subject and we talked about his daughter, Annie, until the battery on my phone died.

I dropped my cellphone onto my bed and began counting the buttons on it. It was a very old phone and I only ever used it for emergencies because I hated being tied to a phone, hated being reachable 24/7. There were so many buttons and they were so small. I had reached twenty-three when Kit sidled into the room and took one look at me and left, but not before she snatched her thigh-length orange sweater from her bed. I idly wondered why a redhead would buy a sweater that clashed so wildly with her hair. Shortly after that, Lucy catapulted into the room, wearing lime-green pants and a leather vest. I barely glanced at her.

"The food in the cafeteria is shitty," she said briskly, "so I'm going to start a catering business for hospitals and we'll serve the best damn food there is, you'll see." The words all ran into each other, so I wasn't sure I had taken in all that she'd said.

"You look like the food," Lucy said next. "Shitty."

I was still in shock.

"I had an ECT," I said tentatively, looking up at her. God, was she beautiful.

"I could have told you that," she said as she paced the room, her energy level higher than a jumping bean, her blonde hair swept back into a jaunty ponytail, her movements lithe and graceful.

"Why didn't you?"

"You didn't ask. Why would you, anyway?" She abruptly stopped pacing and stared at me, her sapphire eyes unreadable.

"You don't remember, do you?"

I shook my head.

"That's okay. Lots of us don't remember," she said sourly, as if she'd just clamped down on a lemon.

"What do you mean?"

"Some patients who have ECT come out afterward with their short-term memories pretty much gone. Even some long-term memories disappear, sometimes for good, although they say they have no real evidence for that. Which is bullshit."

I detected more than a little bit of bitterness in her voice, even though I wasn't paying that much attention to her. I could feel my eyes widening and my skin begin to crawl.

Is that why I had forgotten so much? It wasn't me just losing myself? Someone else had made me lose myself?

I could feel anger surge within me, until another niggling little thought intruded. Maybe the ECT had helped me. After all, I was on the road to recovery. I took a deep breath, amid the cascade of confusing thoughts.

"Have you had one?" I asked Lucy.

"Is the moon far away?" she retorted.

"Did you lose your memory?"

"Some. I didn't know my name, my family, where I was. I felt like my conscious mind had been torn to shreds and all my thoughts were disconnected from each other. Everything seemed new and yet sort of familiar. It sucked. But it didn't last long."

"What do they do to you?"

"You really don't remember, do you?"

"No."

"Electroconvulsive therapy. Or electroshock therapy. That says it all. They put you out cold and paralyze you so that the seizures they create don't end in broken bones. Then they attach electrodes to your head and zap you with electricity. You'd jerk around like a marionette if you weren't paralyzed." Lucy sat down on her bed and tried to bounce up and down on it, a futile effort, because there were no springs.

"It's gross, but at least you're asleep," she went on. "I checked on the Internet before they did it to me. They apply the electric current and watch on the machine you're hooked up to, to see what's going on with your brain. The seizure lasts one and a half to two minutes."

It sounded like torture to me.

"I know what you're thinking," she said, "but it works for a lot of people and not everybody loses their memory."

"Did it work for you?"

"A little bit. They want to try again."

"Will you do it?"

"I don't know. I don't like losing my memory. I just wish there was something a little less like a horror movie, you know? I mean, they don't even really know why it works, when it works. I find that hugely unnerving."

So did I.

chapter ten

It was that lazy time, right after lunch and before any classes started, where everything seemed in limbo. I went to the computer room, a windowless soulless cubbyhole of a room on the men's side of the floor and spent half an hour researching ECT. It wasn't pretty and made me feel ill. It tended to be used only when all other avenues had failed. What did that say about me?

On the way back to my room I went to the bathroom thinking I was going to be sick, and was in the farthest of the three stalls when someone came in and took the stall beside me. Long orange sweater. Kit. Shortly thereafter someone else came in and took the third stall, the one closest to the door. I sat on the toilet seat and stared at the door in front of me. It was pockmarked with paint used to wipe out the graffiti, but someone was ahead of the graffiti police and had scrawled:

I am sinking deep in sin, someone come and push
me in.

The stuff you read in women's cubicles would give
a psychiatrist a lot of thought and the women who
read them no small measure of heartache. I guess that
was why there'd been an attempt to white it out here,
almost as soon as it was written. And if the person who
wrote it was already sinking deep in sin, how could she
be pushed in?

"Damn it!"

The voice came from the first stall and startled me, so
preoccupied was I about sinking into sin.

"Can someone pass me some toilet paper please?"

"Hang on," said Kit. There was a rustling beside me
and then Kit swore.

"Somebody's put the roll on the wrong way. The paper
should fall forward, not backward."

"Oh, it's you," said the voice in the first stall.

"Yeah, it's me."

"Only you would obsess about the toilet paper," said
the voice, dripping sarcasm.

There was a long silence and then Kit said sharply,
"Why are you doing this to me?"

I thought maybe the other person was ignoring the
proffered toilet paper, because what else could Kit mean?
At any rate they obviously got it sorted out because whoever had needed the paper said a brusque "Thank you."

At that point someone else came into the bathroom
to use the shower and my stall mates clammed up. Finally
deciding that I wasn't going to be sick, after all, I exited
the stall and went to wash my hands. As I turned to go I

saw Lucy leaving the first cubicle. Something was definitely going on between her and Kit.

I had chosen to go to the spirituality meeting. The nurses had told me that it was non-denominational and not religious at all. They said it would be soothing for my mind, which definitely needed soothing. So I went.

I should have known better. I should have left the minute I smelled the incense and saw that the lights had been dimmed in the room, trying to hide its ugly utilitarian purpose. Pretty hard to hide the starkness of a windowless conference room, with metal chairs and tables and a bare linoleum floor. I definitely should have left when the group leader introduced herself as a practising Anglican minister, but by then I was curious about how she would keep things non-denominational.

She had arranged the chairs in a circle and had turned on some gentle music. Austin and Bradley were sitting beside each other with Lucy facing them. There were a bunch of others present whose names I didn't know. Some of them were outpatients, but I recognized several from the floor. As I took a seat Jacques walked in and dropped into the empty chair beside me.

"You okay?" he asked, searching my face. I smiled and nodded and the seminar began. Jacques managed to move his leg alongside mine and I could feel the warmth. It made me feel hopeful. Something I thought I had lost. To have feelings again. The minister asked us each in turn whether we had done something just for ourselves today.

"I ate my breakfast," said Austin. It was hard to tell if he was serious or joking. "And I think I've discovered the meaning of life." He paused. For effect? "We live on a giant rubber ball and every time it bounces we have a natural disaster of some kind. The kid who owns the ball sometimes just lets us sit around under the sprinkler and we get floods, or in a closet and it's overcast for days or full of smog and nothing really happens, unless the rats disturb the ball. It's really scary being on the ball as it's screaming toward the ground. There's nowhere to hide and it's just the luck of the draw whether you live or die."

"So the kid's God?" Bradley was looking at Austin with some interest. The fact that he had spoken at all was intriguing.

"You can define it any way you like," said Austin, "but we're just some toy in the big playpen of life." Somebody groaned.

"What's your playground?" said Austin as he stared at Bradley.

"Scientology." Bradley said the word so firmly that it left no doubt about his feelings regarding his chosen belief system. But then his face twitched as if he was annoyed at himself. Why would he be annoyed? I wondered what the odds were that there would be two Scientologists on a psychiatric ward, let alone one. Mavis and Bradley. Lucy whistled softly and Leo moaned. The rest of us just stared.

"Then what the hell are you doing here?" said Austin. "I thought Scientologists believe psychiatry is a destructive force and shouldn't exist?" I was impressed. I hadn't known that. Austin was full of information.

"Sometimes you have to downplay your principles to get what you need," said Bradley as he stared down Austin.

"Oh, my God," said Austin. "What the hell does that mean?"

But before Bradley could say anything else the minister intervened. "We're getting off topic here. Bradley, what have you done for yourself today?"

Bradley just stared at the minister as though she was some alien creature. She patiently went around the circle then and didn't get much out of anybody, including me, until she came to Jacques.

"I've decided I don't need to follow most of the twelve steps of Alcoholics Anonymous and I feel good about that. It's a load off my back."

The minister blinked several times and then cleared her throat. She looked a little lost.

"Is there a reason?" she finally asked.

"I'm an atheist. Six of the twelve steps refer directly to God." Talk about throwing down the gauntlet. What was he trying to do? Start a religious war? And this was supposed to be non-denominational.

"Even though you don't believe, you can still believe in yourself. Know that you are unique and that the choices you make define you. You don't have to believe in God to follow the steps. You just have to believe in yourself."

"And you're saying that to people who routinely hallucinate and have delusions? How do you believe in yourself if you don't know what's real and what isn't half the time? Like the Norse gods, the Greek gods, the Christian god, Scientology's supreme being, and all the other gods. What's real?" He looked directly at Bradley, as if he was trying to bait him, but Bradley stayed mute.

"God is a delusion, anyway, created to make us feel better about dying," said Jacques, the tone of his voice clearly confrontational.

"Sometimes death seems like heaven," said Lucy, as if she hadn't understood Jacques at all. "When you're depressed and then manic and back and forth like me, it's like having your mind plunged into a swirling fog, so that sometimes things are clear, and sometimes they are not."

She was staring at the floor and her hands were pulling at a frayed patch on her jeans. She went on, "And hidden in the haze are these big pieces of darkness that grab the mind and spin it like a top, into despair, hopeless, desolate despair, and it hides any possible avenue of escape."

She was speaking in a monotone, her face hidden. "And then one day your mind comes out of the fog and becomes excited, with one idea after the other bombarding you. The thoughts are so many and so strong that you can't concentrate on any particular one and you get impatient with people who try to point this out to you."

Now she looked up. "You speak so quickly that people have a hard time understanding you and that makes you more and more impatient." Her words were running into each other. "You have no fear, none at all. You can go out on a lake in the middle of a horrible lightning storm and know you won't die. It leads you to do some very dangerous things, because like pain, you need fear to tell you you're in danger."

She stopped talking and we all sat there thinking about what she had said. It was disquieting to me to realize that I understood some of what she was saying, not just superficially, but deep down, way deep down.

"Mavis died."

I swivelled my head toward Austin. Everybody did, including the minister, who at this point probably thought she'd jumped out of the frying pan into the fire.

"No, she didn't," the minister said gently.

"Yes, she did."

"Why are you so sure?"

"Because I killed her," said Austin with a triumphant look on his face.

Austin took off before I could pigeonhole him about his astounding confession, so I went in search of him and found myself in the cafeteria. The tables each had six chairs neatly tucked in under them, with a little tray of condiments placed dead centre. The bare linoleum floors were polished like a mirror and the empty pale-green walls screamed institution. The humungous television set, covered in Plexiglas, was tuned to some sports channel. I wondered how many TVs had been smashed by patients before they put the Plexiglas on. At first I thought the room was empty until I noticed the top of a head poking out from behind one of the overstuffed green sofas that dominated the room — the beginnings of a bald head. Thinning hair. Austin.

I cleared my throat so I wouldn't scare him half to death and walked around the sofa. He was sitting with his head bowed, chin on his chest. He'd looked exactly like that the last time I had talked to him here. He didn't look up when I took a seat across from him. We sat in silence for several minutes, or at least it felt like several minutes. It was probably only a few seconds, but I was bursting with impatience.

"How did you kill her?"

He looked up then, his eyes foggy.

"She was a menace," he said, and lapsed back into silence.

Not exactly the answer to my question. "Why?" I tried next. His eyes shifted from my right shoulder to the window.

"She was an alien. She came from the future to steal our past. She had to be stopped."

My heart sank.

"So you killed her."

"So I killed her."

"How did you do it, Austin?" I asked again. I felt like a ghoul, asking such a question, but I was curious. Maybe I was grasping at straws, but no matter how bizarre his story might seem there was always a chance that there was a kernel of truth to it. I just had to find that kernel.

"Her friends tried to take me with them. They surrounded my bed, their eyes burning into my soul, and I nearly let myself go. They were so strong." He sat up further, his gaze still on the window.

I followed his gaze, as if I could see what he was seeing.

"But they decided they didn't want me. Can you believe that?" He turned to look at me then, and I shrugged, not knowing what to say.

"They didn't *want* me," he said again. "So I got up out of bed. It was really quiet. I had almost like a sixth sense. The one that senses nothing. Nothing at all. The dead sense. Death is an abstract; it doesn't really exist, except in my mind. We are just a continuation of matter. We die and parts of us are eaten by bacteria and maggots and parts of us are ground to dust. But every molecule is taken up by something else and we become billions of different fragmented things, like a kaleidoscope of ourselves. The bug that eats my baby finger incorporates me into it and then shits some of me out and I go on to the next adventure."

He had lost the train of thought that I was interested in, so I said, "You got out of bed and ..."

His eyes turned back to me, hazy and unfocused. I didn't know if it was his meds that were turning his eyes to fog or his schizophrenia. Maybe it was both.

"It's hard to get out of bed sometimes. The voices don't like me to rearrange my soul. They want me to do exactly what they say."

"And what did they say this time?"

"To get out of bed. It was urgent that I warn Mavis."

"Warn her about what?"

"That she was going to die."

"But you killed her. Why would you warn her?"

"Because the voices didn't tell me to kill her until I started to warn her."

"What did you do?"

"I got out of bed," said Austin, and shut up.

I was having a hard time controlling my impatience. "And then what?"

Austin laughed. "Do you know how easy it is to break down all the barricades they put up here?"

I nodded my encouragement, not knowing what the hell he was talking about.

"The nurses always leave the door unlocked at night between the men's side and the women's side — fire regulations, I guess — so it was easy to get to Mavis's room. The halls were empty, just the way the voices said they would be. Aren't you going to ask me how I knew which bed Mavis was in?"

"How did you know?" I obliged, still tamping down my growing impatience.

"She told me, of course. Don't you know anything?"

He'd been hunched over, hugging his elbows, looking up at me from a closed protective posture. Now suddenly he sat back and gestured with both his chubby arms, like a traffic cop.

"Bed closest to the door, closest to the cafeteria. Door was open. A cinch, they said it would be. All I had to do was tap her on the shoulder and warn her. They were going to do the rest."

"But they didn't." I forced myself to take a deep breath. If I lost my patience I could lose him.

"No. They didn't. I was leaning over her when they told me to kill her. She had thrown her covers off and she was wearing her crossword-puzzle pajamas and her tiny silver cross around her neck and I thought it would be neat if I could only make up some clues for her pajamas. Good clues. The kind that when you get them you feel really good about yourself. Not like the clues that turn into red-bellied demons trying to eat your mind. But they chanted it over and over. *Kill her. Kill her. Kill her.* So insistent. Her pillow was so soft, you know. She brought it especially from home. So soft. She didn't even struggle. Did you know the mentally ill are no more prone to violence than anyone else?"

And then he smiled at me — or at the non sequitur.

"You know, I'm perfectly sane most of the time," he said. "I just have my moments."

After I left Austin I bumped into Jacques near the nursing station. He led me partway down the hall and leaned his massive frame against the painted cinderblock wall, hands in pockets. He had such a presence, kind of intimidating and kind of exciting. I wondered if maybe he was a bodyguard in real life. He was certainly built for it. I had never felt particularly small before, but I did with him. Was that what excited me about him?

"Did you know Bradley was a Scientologist?" I asked as I leaned up against the wall beside him. He moved closer to me, so that his arm touched mine.

"No, but it's interesting, isn't it?"

He pushed against me and nearly knocked me over. He reached out and steadied me and I suddenly realized that when he had kissed me I hadn't tasted smoke. Smoke or no smoke, it was really hard to concentrate on what he was saying. But I made a brave effort.

"Do you know much about Scientology?" he asked.

"Not really," I said. I knew that Scientology had stirred up a lot of controversy lately, had a couple of movie-star adherents, but that was about it. I'd never paid it much attention.

"Well," said Jacques, "I looked it up on Wikipedia and it was started in 1952 by the science fiction and fantasy writer L. Ron Hubbard. In a nutshell, Scientologists believe in the reincarnation of *thetans* or souls. These thetans spend time on other planets before coming to earth."

"It sounds like a delusion, but then so do other religions, this one arguably weirder than most," I said.

"Exactly," said Jacques. "I'd say it's heaven-sent for schizophrenics, who are already seeing and hearing things. They might just see it as a confirmation of their own hallucinations or delusions. Kindred spirits, so to speak. And easy to recruit. For any religion."

Jacques pushed himself away from the wall and pulled his hands out of his pockets. I couldn't help but notice a telltale white mark where a wedding ring used to be. I pulled my wandering mind back to the topic at hand.

"Bradley didn't exactly defend his religion, did he?" said Jacques.

"What are you getting at?"

"Maybe he didn't want us to know he was a Scientologist, but just revealed it in the heat of the moment."

I thought back to the twitch I'd seen on Bradley's face.

"Why wouldn't he want us to know that?" I asked.

"Because it loosely links him to Mavis."

"Mavis and Bradley," I said.

"Yeah. Mavis and Bradley. What kind of coincidence would bring two Scientologists, who are also schizo-phrenic, to a mental hospital?" he said. "Especially when Austin said Scientologists believe psychiatry should be abolished." Jacques reached into his pocket and pulled out a box of toothpicks.

"Might be a motive there somewhere," I ventured.

"You think?" he said, but there was a smile in his eyes as he said it.

We fell into silence. When neither of us could imme-diately come up with any great motive he said, "Okay, so who else could have murdered her? Who had easy access?" He fiddled with the box of toothpicks, trying to get one out.

I debated about telling him about Austin, but I just wasn't sure about his story. It seemed so surreal, so I kept my counsel. Instead I said, "Kit and I and Lucy shared Mavis's room. Any one of us could have got up in the night and strangled her with the scarf."

"Let's assume you're not the murderer, Cordi. Lucy and Kit are the most plausible ones. We have to see if we can find motives for them." He finally got a toothpick out and put it in his mouth.

"How do we do that?" I asked.

"Engage them in conversation, ask the right questions and see what happens."

"That sounds a lot easier said than done," I said.

"Okay. How easy would it be for Bradley or Austin or Leo to sneak in and kill her while you were sleeping?"

"Certainly possible. The meds they give Kit and me and Lucy make us sleep pretty soundly."

"So you're saying anyone on the floor could have done it?"

I nodded. "That includes all the other patients on the floor, besides our small group."

"Yeah, but it's likely the killer knew Mavis and isn't just an acquaintance," said Jacques.

"How can you be so sure?"

"I can't, but we have to start somewhere and I say we start with those people who knew Mavis. Can we eliminate anybody?"

"The nurses not on duty."

"Who was on duty for your room that night."

I thought back.

"Ella did a double shift. So she had access."

"What about the other nurses?"

"I don't know."

"Leaves us with a lot of suspects and no motives. Lucy or Kit could have cheeked their meds and got up in the night and murdered her. Leo or Bradley or Austin could have sneaked past the nursing station and killed her. So could I, for that matter. It can be a pretty deserted ward in the middle of the night. Dicey though."

I looked at Jacques with new eyes. Why was he so interested and why did he believe me so blindly? I felt a cold tendril of fear weasel its way into my brain and I shivered. I just didn't want him to turn out to be a murderer.

chapter eleven

I was standing on the subway platform. It was midday and there were only two other people waiting for the train. I could see the black hole of the tunnel and feel the drafts of wind announcing a train. I looked in the other direction and saw Lucy and Kit, Jacques, Leo, Austin, Ella, Dr. Osborn, and Bradley marching toward me like a vanquishing army. They were expressionless and zombielike. I started backing up. Their eyes were unblinking, reptilian, as they advanced on me. I could hear the train coming as they engulfed me, pushing me toward the edge, the screaming of the brakes, the breathless horror, before the train struck....

I woke up gasping for air, experienced that horrible surreal moment when you are not sure if the dream was real or not. I lay sweating in bed for a long time, aware only that I was afraid and felt powerless against it. I forced myself to sit up on the side of my bed and felt a momentary wave of dizziness sweep through me, unnerving me. I sat still, listening to the hum of the furnace and watching the red light of the smoke alarm silently flashing on and off, on and off. It was mesmerizing and I succumbed to its easy seduction.

But only for a while. And then my fear returned. Someone was trying to kill me, and not only did I not know for sure who it was, although Ella seemed a good bet, but I wasn't really very clear on the motive. Was it because I was the only one who knew for sure that Mavis was dead, or thought I knew for sure that Mavis was dead? What threat was that? Unless there was more to it than her death. Unless the reason she died was important to keep secret. *Could that be it?* I wondered.

I stood up in the dim light from the window and looked outside. Even at this late hour I could see a man brushing the snow off his car. I looked at the time — 3 a.m. Perhaps this was about the time that Mavis died. I poked my feet into some slippers and peered out the door, which we sometimes left open for ventilation. I opened it wide. No squeaky hinges, no sound at all. I looked both ways up and down the hall. Not a soul in sight. I stepped into the hall, carefully holding on to the knob and easing the door shut behind me. The hall lights were dimmed — was that to make it feel more homey or to save electricity?

Feeling like an idiot, unsure of what I was doing, I flattened myself against the wall as I sidled down the hall toward the nursing station. I poked my head up above the wainscotting so that I could look in the window. There were two doors into the station, one from the men's side and one from the women's side. Ella was sitting at one of the computers and quietly laughing at something she was reading on the screen. Didn't know she could laugh. One nurse, 3:00 a.m. How easy it was to be about with no one noticing. I was about to leave when the far door began to open. I crouched down below the wainscotting and waited. Although I couldn't see I was able to make out some of the words.

"Bloody hell … refused the …"

"Need … help."

There was silence for a while and then, "Is it true … say about Mavis?" I strained so hard to hear the words.

"… scarf … peaceful … strange."

"Like … the others?"

"Maybe … shock."

"Weird."

"Yeah."

They stopped talking after that and when I looked, Ella had gone back to her computer and whoever she'd been talking to was nowhere in sight. It seemed like a really boring job, the night shift in a psychiatric ward, but only if something didn't go wrong.

I crept back down that long deserted hallway, feeling like a grain of sand lost on the beach. What had they meant by "others"?

I awoke the next morning feeling like a piece of dirt. I had a throbbing headache and my mind was groggy. Kit tried to sort of tidy me out of bed by making my bed with me in it. I looked at the time: 8:15. Breakfast, and I could not get myself out of bed. Total inertia. What was the point anyway? To eat? To survive? You need a point to your life to want to get up and I couldn't find that point.

Kit tried to cajole me and Lucy tried to bully me, but eventually they left for breakfast and I lay there waiting for the inevitable nurse to come and get me. But then I remembered Mavis. And it took my mind off myself for some precious seconds. What had happened to her? How had she died? Why had she died? I was contemplating these questions when Ella breezed into the room. She looked awful, with big bags under her eyes. Maybe the night shift wasn't all that easy. In any other circumstances I would have felt sorry for her, but how do you feel sorry for someone you suspect is trying to kill you?

"You know the rules," she said. "Breakfast means breakfast, so let's get out of bed now, shall we?"

When I didn't move, she said in a soft voice that just sounded menacing to me, "What's wrong?"

I didn't answer.

"Look, I know some days are a bitch and you just can't get out of bed, but you know that you'll feel better once you get up."

It didn't help that she had a point. I was arguably better once I got up, but the getting up was sometimes so hard.

"Come on," she said. "Let's go."

Why was she being so nice? She helped me get out of bed and even found me my clothes.

"There's always light at the end of the tunnel, even if you can't see it."

She didn't wait for me to get dressed, but she did wait until I was out of bed. As she left she smiled and said, "Dr. Osborn wants to see you at ten o'clock," and then she was gone, diabolical smile and all. I went back to bed.

Sometime later someone came into the room. I couldn't see who it was because I had the covers pulled up over my head. The rummaging sounds were coming from Kit's bed. After a while someone else came into the room, but no one said anything. The rummaging stopped and I heard the shuffling of feet. Even as down as I was, my curiosity got the better of me and I peeked out from under the covers.

Not what I expected to see. Lucy and Kit were standing with their arms entwined around each other in a silent embrace. *Guess they made up*, I thought. Some second sense made them realize they had an audience and they quickly let go of each other and moved apart. I gave them a few seconds to get their acts together and then pushed back the covers and sat up. What was it that had passed between them? Simple friendship or was it more than that? Something was going on. I remembered the conversation in the bathroom. Maybe it hadn't been just the toilet paper that Kit had been talking about. I finally got dressed and went to see if the kitchen staff had left any food out. Orange juice. Coffee. Nothing else. I got myself a coffee, then went and sat by the window overlooking the city. I could see the streetcars moving slowly along the snow-clogged street. Pedestrians had their heads down as they battled the wind and the snow. It seemed so strange to be warm and dry with my coffee and my sofa, while a mere quarter inch of glass separated me from the miserable cold.

It was Dr. Osborn himself who found me staring out the window at the blowing snow.

"You know what they say about snowflakes, don't you?" he asked.

I knew he was just being friendly — no two are the same — but I wasn't feeling particularly friendly, so I said nothing. He inclined his head and I slowly got up and followed him through the door to his office.

This time he had wind chimes as background music, and the moment that I walked from the corridor into his office everything was muted by his thick carpet. It was like walking into a movie set from the bare bones of a hangar. Totally different world. I sat down on the sofa, as far from him as possible.

He placed a file folder on his desk, picked up another, and walked over to the chair opposite me. I came straight to the point.

"What did you mean by 'another ECT'?" I asked.

He flipped through some pages in the folder and then looked at me above his glasses.

"You don't remember the first?" He took off his glasses.

I asked him all the questions I had asked my brother and got all the same answers. That I had been too severely depressed to give permission myself and that my brother had consented.

I sat there in that strange cocoon of a room, with the soothing music and the ghosts of all the pained patients who had sat here before me, and I wondered how this could have happened to me.

"What did you do to me?" I asked softly.

He more or less walked me through what Lucy had told me. The paralysis. The electrodes. The shock. The seizure lasting about ninety seconds.

"And what about my memory?"

"It's just short term. It'll come back."

"It doesn't for everybody," I said.

He sighed. "Yes, you're right. A few unfortunate people lose short-term memory and even some long-term memories, but most do not, and I emphasize *most*."

I stared at him and cleared my throat.

"I looked it up on the Internet," I said. "My research says it can be as high as thirty percent. Three out of every ten people. That's still a lot."

He had the decency to look down at his file folder and then said, "It helped you, Cordi. It pulled you out. If you go back to that place, you need to consider having another." He tapped the folder against his knee and I could almost see his thoughts forming. I was about to say, *Yeah, but at what cost?* when he surprised me and said, "Would you like to go home for an overnight visit tomorrow, if you feel up to it? Do you good."

When I didn't answer, he added, "It's important for you to reconnect with your outside life as soon as possible, and you have made some progress — the depression has lifted. However, I'm worried about your preoccupation with Mavis, and we need to address that."

Just then, the phone rang. He stood up and went over to his desk to answer it, dropping my folder on top of a pile of others.

It appeared there was some mix-up with meds on the floor and he asked me to wait while he cleared it up. He closed the door behind him so quietly I had to watch to make sure he had really gone. I got up from the sofa and crossed to his desk.

There were a lot of research papers on the desk, all with Richard Osborn as co-author with David Ellison. So *that* was his first name. The papers ran the gamut from CBT studies to medical interventions for Alzheimer's patients and memory loss. I wondered how he had time to do so much research and attend to all his patients, as well.

I was torn between looking at his research and leafing through my folder, which he'd left on his desk. My folder won. I was officially patient number 1356 in large red letters and my entire medical history was listed in great detail, including my ECT treatment. I flipped through it and saw where he'd first decided I was a candidate for ECT and where he'd got Ryan's permission. I noticed some of the other folders on his desk and my heart lurched when I saw that one of the folders was Mavis's. I was about to pick it up when Osborn's voice cut the air.

"Do you always snoop like that, Cordi?" His voice was cold and even.

I turned to him, my own folder still in my hand and said, "It is my understanding that my medical history belongs to me."

He didn't say anything. He just came up to me and took the folder from my hand.

"And did you find anything in there of interest to you?" he asked.

I shook my head. I thought he was going to end the session right then and there, but instead he returned to the topic of my "obsession" with Mavis again. He had nothing new to tell me, however, and I guess I had nothing new to tell him. Nothing I *wanted* to tell him, anyway.

chapter twelve

Like Austin, I had my moments too. Mostly just a stomach-clenching fear that the depression would come back. Otherwise I felt pretty good. The fact that I seemed to be collecting clues without too much trouble meant that my mind was on the mend, even though some of my memories were missing, at least according to Ryan and Dr. Osborn. But really, how could I tell if I wasn't remembering something I'd forgotten? I went to another cognitive behavioural therapy class just to get away from my room and to see if I could find out anything more about Mavis, but it was all dead ends.

I was feeling restless and irritable, so I left the hospital and walked the hundred feet or so to Tim Hortons for a coffee. I was lucky and found a table by the window. There was a guy standing outside dressed only in a T-shirt, blocking my view as he hurriedly inhaled on a cigarette. I marvelled at the strength of his addiction. It was bitterly cold outside.

"Hi, Cordi."

I looked up in annoyance to find Kit gazing down at me, one hand holding a steaming cup of coffee and the other a doughnut in a wad of napkins. She asked if I minded if she joined me. I minded very much. I was feeling very antisocial, but I still had enough social grace to realize I couldn't say no without hurting her feelings, and enough compassion to care. So I waved her to a seat. And then said nothing. It was childish, but I felt trapped.

I watched as she carefully placed her coffee on the table and then wiped off the chair, before wiping off the tabletop with one of her napkins. Then she sat down and folded her used napkin into a tiny little square and looked at me expectantly.

"You don't eat doughnuts?" she asked.

What a conversation starter, I thought. I didn't feel like telling her about my taste in doughnuts, so I shook my head. She took another napkin and wiped the rim of her cup before taking a sip. She then reached across the table and wiped a spot of coffee that had dribbled off my mug to the tabletop. I resisted the impulse to slap her hand.

"Why do you come here if you have to clean everything before you sit down, or eat or drink?" It was a pointed antisocial question.

"I don't do it because I want to. I don't choose to be obsessive compulsive," she said, her voice a bit cold and very apprehensive. "I can't help it. Even my name, spelled backward sort of, labels me, because my obsessions and rituals are really just *tics* of the mind." She took a sip of coffee. I wondered if she had thought of the other meaning for Kit spelled backward. Methamphetamine. I figured it would be unkind to tell her.

"I worry so much that my mother will die if I step on a single line. It tears me apart, the anxiety is so bad. I can hardly breathe sometimes. Intellectually I know it's obsessive, but I can't help myself. The worry is overwhelming and forces me to do all these rituals to defuse things."

"Like you and Lucy." *Talk about a non sequitur.*

"What about me and Lucy?" Kit's voice dropped an octave.

"Are you close friends?"

"We get along."

"But not all the time."

I waited, but she suddenly got up and went to the bathroom without saying a word. When she got back I stared at her, but she just stared into her coffee.

"Did you hear or see anything the night Mavis died?" I said, switching topics.

She looked up at me quickly. "What do you mean?" She sounded defensive and looked really uncomfortable.

"She died in our room. I just wanted to know if you saw anything."

"Why do you keep saying she died? The hospital people say she didn't. Besides, I was asleep. I wouldn't have seen anything," she said.

Avoiding my eyes, she gathered up her things and left me to contemplate the remains of my coffee and the nature of Kit's and Lucy's relationship and whether it had any bearing on Mavis.

It wasn't until 9:00 p.m. — medication roll call — that anything of interest happened. When I arrived, all the chairs outside the dispensary were taken and so I took up my position leaning against the wall, some distance from the medication room. I fervently hoped that Ella wasn't dispensing the drugs, because I really did want to get better and that meant taking my medication. Cheeking it too often was not a good idea if I wanted to keep seeing the light at the end of the tunnel, and I'd been cheeking it a lot because Ella was dispensing. I still wasn't taking any chances.

I was leaning with my back against the wall and staring at a notice on the wall across from me. It was a notice I'd read the previous night, something about warning the nurses ahead of time if you were leaving the unit for a night or two, so they could get your medication to you. But now there was something written in pen in the space below the words of the notice. It hadn't been there the night before, I was certain. I crossed the hall to get a better look and then wished I hadn't.

> My desolate mind cannot erase
> The darkness within … it's God's disgrace.
> There's not much left but a splintered soul
> Why won't my psyche let me be whole …

It was so plaintive, so sad. The mental pain, the emotional pain, the brain pain that anybody who has ever been there will understand, screamed its message from this poem written on a hospital wall, outside the dispensary for the drugs designed to ease the pain. Drugs that didn't always work.

It wasn't Ella tonight. It was some nurse I didn't know. She opened the split door to the dispensary. It was little more than a glorified closet. She closed the bottom half of the door and left the upper half open. As she called our names we went and got our medication. It was all pre-packaged in individual doses by the pharmacy downstairs, and it was her job to punch out each bubble-wrapped pill, place it in a little paper cup, and give it to us to take while she watched. There were a lot of people ahead of me and I started to pace up and down the hallway, staring at the speckled linoleum floor. Up and down, up and down. A nurse came and stopped by the notice, apparently reading the poem. I watched her take it down and leave. Up and down, up and down. I even caught myself pulling a Kit — I began to avoid the lines of the linoleum squares.

"You're going to wear out the floor if you're not careful."

I stopped pacing and looked in the direction of the voice. Jacques was lounging against the wall and I wondered how long he'd been there. I certainly hadn't noticed him. Although he was quite noticeable, dressed all in black with his blond hair cascading around his massive shoulders, his mischievous green eyes dancing like wildfire. He pushed himself away from the wall with one smooth fluid motion and met me halfway.

"Anything new?" he asked. I hesitated and then decided to tell him about Austin, just to get it off my chest.

"I talked to Austin."

"And?"

"I don't think he's the murderer." I told Jacques what Austin had told me about killing Mavis.

"So why don't you think it was Austin?"

"He didn't mention the red scarf once and his language sounded delusional, as if he had seen it in his head and nothing more."

"And it's rare for schizophrenics to get violent."

"Exactly, and he didn't mention the scarf and his story seemed so surreal. If you accept the premise that she was an alien bent on stealing his past, then murdering her has some logic to it. But it sounded so much like a dream, a nightmare haunting a man whose mind is not well...."

My voice trailed off as I thought about how hard it is to live inside a mind that is ill, and that delusions can kill.

"You okay?" he asked, looking intently at me.

He liked to ask me that. I wondered if that was some reflection on me. Did I always appear not okay to him? I pulled myself back from my thoughts and said, "Well, I know why my memory has been so bad."

He cocked a blond eyebrow at me and I told him about the ECT I couldn't remember. Not sure why, but it seemed harmless. He was very interested and asked me all sorts of questions about Osborn and the protocol for ECT and all about memory loss, until I finally said, "Look, I don't really remember. Why are you so interested?"

He seemed nonplussed at first by my question, but then replied, "When I was really depressed Dr. Osborn suggested ECT, but I shied away. Coward, I guess. Got right into the room and everything before I changed my mind. I'm glad I did. My treatment seems to be working without imperiling my brain."

He moved closer to me and made me momentarily forget what we were talking about.

"Did it help you? Even if you don't remember?" he asked gently.

I shook my head and then nodded it, then shook it again, alternating the two motions, making him laugh.

It was my turn to query him.

"What do alcoholics do if they are not religious?"

"You don't mince words."

"It's just a continuation of what you said in CBT." I was fishing but I wasn't sure for what. Or why.

He stared at me, his gaze strong and unwavering. "They don't go to AA," he said simply.

When I didn't respond to that, he added, "What can I say? I'm not religious. I will not turn myself 'over to the care of God' or 'believe that a Power greater than ourselves could restore us to sanity,' quote unquote. I will not submit to a myth."

"How does an atheist alcoholic get help, then?"

"This atheist alcoholic has a good doctor and a good CBT program and supportive friends. It seems to be working."

I wasn't quite sure what to say to that. Was it his wishful thinking or was it really working? Why did I think his answers were too pat — as if he had rehearsed them?

"What's your poison?" I asked abruptly.

Jacques hesitated. "Scotch," he finally said.

I glanced down the hall and saw that the lineup was shortening, but neither of us made any effort to join it.

"I overheard Ella and another nurse talking about Mavis," I said. I filled Jacques in on what I had overheard — the scarf, shock, others.

Jacques homed in on the same thing I had. "What did she mean by 'others'?"

"I don't know, but my imagination says it can't be good."

Jacques looked at me shrewdly. "You think there've been other murders?"

I nodded.

"You have quite an imagination," he said.

But he didn't refute it.

chapter thirteen

———————————————————

Because Ella wasn't on duty I took my meds. I was beginning to doubt myself where she was concerned. There had been no further attempts on my life and no telling glances in my direction. I put her out of my mind.

Most people had drifted off to bed when I went to the common room to snag a juice and some toast. I was waiting for the toast to pop up when Leo sidled into the room and nodded at me. He picked up a juice and then looked at the toaster. I could almost see the wheels of his mind turning and knew he wanted the toaster and wished I wasn't there. The way the shadows played across his face made him seem ghoulish in a Dickensian sort of way, the bags under his eyes drooping down his cheeks, his chin drooping into his neck. He reached across me to get a piece of bread, his long skeletal fingers an extension of his gangly arms and tall spaghetti-thin frame. My toast popped up and I took it and placed it on my plate. In a flash he had his piece in the toaster and was reaching to press down the lever.

I was desperately trying to find a way to start a conversation with him to see what he knew about Mavis and blurted, "Were you and Mavis friends?"

His hand froze above the lever and his entire body tensed as if I had tasered him. In a preternaturally quiet and controlled voice he said, "Please don't talk about her."

I should have listened, but I was so intent on ferreting out clues that I failed to heed his distress. "You must have known her," I said. "You were here before I came and so was she."

He turned to look at me and I almost jumped away from him. For a moment his eyes registered wild panic, but then he turned away from me and left abruptly, leaving his untoasted bread behind. That was the moment Ella came into the room. She turned to watch Leo shuffling hurriedly down the hall, then looked at me.

"What did you say to him?" she asked. The implication was clear. It was my fault Leo was upset.

"I asked him if he and Mavis were friends." Ella closed her eyes momentarily, as if gathering her patience.

"He doesn't like to talk about Mavis," she said.

"Why not?" I asked.

She smiled and shook her head. "You know we can't talk about patients."

Yeah, I knew, and it was frustrating as hell.

Morning came quickly. I would be spending the night at home, and it felt good not to be dreading it. I was actually looking forward to my own space. I didn't tell Ryan. I didn't want him to worry about me or, worse, feel obligated to invite me to stay with him and his family again.

I loved his family, but his kids, little Davey and Annie, if she was there, would be too much for me for a while yet. I didn't want them catching me in an unguarded moment of sadness or despair and I knew I wasn't strong enough yet to put up a front for so many hours. At the hospital it was different. I could be depressed without anyone trying to cheer me up. I could be myself, knowing that the doctors and nurses were there to rescue me if things got too bad.

All my good intentions to leave after lunch got way-laid when I fell asleep and woke up to find the sun had already set. I was doing a lot of sleeping. I knew that. And it altered my sense of time so that occasionally I wasn't immediately sure what time of day it was or even what day. On top of that, the ward life had a way of blurring time for me even further, with one day merging into the next.

Fifteen minutes later I found myself on the subway again. I could have taken a taxi, but I didn't feel like talking to anyone. I wanted to be anonymous. Besides, it was snowing hard and the streets were slippery. Traffic would be a bitch. I stood well back from the platform edge as I waited for the train. It was full and I had to squeeze myself in for five stops before the train spat me out and I caught the bus.

The falling snow coated everything, making it diffi-cult to see more than twenty feet ahead and muffling all sound. I got off the bus at its most distant stop and then had a ten-minute walk home past Chorley Park with its black naked trees partially lit by strategically placed street lamps. I reached Governor's Bridge and, as I always do, I stopped and looked down the snow-covered street to the far side. It always made me feel lonely, this bridge spanning a wooded ravine. The place was eerie. Timeless. Especially at night with the old-fashioned street lights casting their glow in the darkness.

The railings bracketing the bridge and the sidewalks were actually shoulder-high walls of cement a foot thick and into which thousands upon thousands of pebbles had been pressed, making it feel like some giant's sandpaper. The walls were pierced every three inches by narrow slits the shape of cathedral windows, which allowed children and shorter people to peer through to the tree-covered ravine sixty feet below. Taller people could peer over the top of the wall, and stupidly adventurous people could even sit on it.

Looking down that bridge, partially obscured by the swirling snow, made me feel as though I were living in another century, when the streetlights were gas lamps and the vehicles we drove were powered by horses. It was deserted. No one had driven down the bridge for a while, as there were no tire tracks. The sidewalk was pristine, too. I started to cross the bridge. It was so soft and quiet I could have been the last person on earth.

Except I wasn't.

Suddenly someone grabbed me from behind, lifted me up, and threw me over the bridge.

chapter fourteen

I tried to save myself, reaching wildly out into space, searching for the solid comfort of the wall. I hadn't had time to even realize it wasn't there before I felt something grabbing at my coat from a dozen different directions, the sharp jabs almost penetrating my coat. The noise they made was the sharp crack of frozen wood.

The tree stood just a few feet shy of the height of the bridge and its branches slowed my descent, until they finally stopped me momentarily, leaving me dangling precariously on a branch that was too small to hold my weight for long. I gasped as it gave way.

I fell down through the tree, breaking more and bigger branches as I went, all the while wildly reaching out to grab hold of something, anything. And finally I did. A branch as thick as my wrist took my weight as it bent toward the ground, which I did not dare look at, for fear the motion might make me lose my grip.

The branch let me down ever so gently onto a good

solid limb, which I immediately straddled and then hugged like a long-lost friend. As soon as I knew I was safe I turned to look up at the bridge and froze.

There was a hooded figure looking down at me, silhouetted by the light of the street lamp. I panicked. Whoever it was knew I was alive, and I was a sitting duck. I had to get down before my assailant got to me. It was so snowy that there was no depth perception, but I could see where the dark bark of the tree trunk disappeared beneath the snow, or at least I thought I could. For all I knew the snow I saw was swirling snow and air, not sitting on hard ground. Panicked as I was, I didn't want to cripple myself in a fall, for then I'd have no chance to escape. But I had so little time. Even now my attacker would be running along the bridge to the edge and then down the steep embankment of the ravine.

I was wearing my bulky calf-length coat and as I tried to climb down to the next limb, it caught my legs and I almost fell. I was going to have to jump if I had any hope of escaping my would-be killer. I straddled the limb again and quickly took off my coat, holding on to the limb with one hand and sort of shaking out of it. I was thankful I at least had a sweater on, but the wind went right through it and I knew I had to be quick. I had to be smart, too. I rolled the coat into a ball and tied it together with its hood ties. Then I dropped the coat in a spot that appeared to have the fewest branches from where I was sitting and watched it, holding my breath, praying it would land, and not get caught by a branch.

It didn't get caught and now it lay on the ground, a visual reference for how high up I was.

Maybe ten feet.

I could jump that.

So I did and landed in knee-deep snow. I pitched forward into a roll and then stood up and whipped my head around to look at the ravine embankment a hundred feet away. The dark figure was floundering down the slope, skidding and slipping through the snow, but making good time. I turned and started running toward the other end of the bridge, the other side of the ravine, although my movement could not exactly be called "running." The heavy mashed-potato snow sucked at my legs with every step and too soon my legs began to burn with the effort. I kept turning to look back, even though I knew that slowed me down. My attacker kept gaining on me and I was getting a bit light-headed from the panic that threatened to throttle me. I wondered if my legs would hold out or betray me.

By the time I got to the embankment my attacker was fifty feet back and closing. I realized with dismay that I was breaking trail for whomever it was. The embankment was steep and I kept slipping, but I clawed my way up that hill until my legs were screaming. I came out through someone's back yard, at the edge of the bridge, and saw a couple not too far away walking their dog. I was too winded to cry out, but I forced my wobbly legs into a staggering run until I was twenty feet from the couple.

I looked behind me again. I could see my pursuer, a shadowy hooded figure, standing now on the road to the bridge, silently watching me. I had almost caught up with the couple, and when I turned one last time, I could see my would-be killer walking away from me back over the bridge, just a shape, really, moving on the sidewalk under the streetlamps. I stood and watched until the figure was out of sight. I stared at the bridge. It looked exactly the same as it always had. Nothing had changed. It still looked eerie and timeless, and endlessly indifferent.

It wasn't a long walk through the falling snow to my home at Governor's Manor, but it was long enough for my sweat to cool and my body to chill. Governor's Manor was exactly what it said it was, a manor, but it had been renovated into a row of condominium town-homes. The manor looked like a long, two-storey, stately home with a white-stucco exterior, crisscrossed with black wooden trim, multiple peaked roofs, and in the summer a lush garden on either side of a circular drive. My place was a two-bedroom overlooking the driveway. I walked through the alcove to my front door and could barely make my frozen fingers insert the key into the lock and open the door.

I kicked off my wet boots and started peeling off my clothes as I walked through my open-concept living room to the master bedroom and bathroom beyond. I ran a hot bath and lay there soaking up the warmth. My mind, however, remained cold and numb.

Someone had almost killed me. Again. Would have, save for the tree. I tried to think back, to review the sequence of events, but there was nothing to indicate who had done this to me. No indication that it had been Ella. No indication that it hadn't been. I didn't know what to do. On the one hand, if I called the police, what could they do? There was no evidence to be found. On the other hand, if it was my assailant's second attempt, there was no reason not to believe that there would be a third, and maybe final, attempt. Final for me, that is. So I called the police.

It was no longer an emergency situation, since I was safely home, so they didn't arrive on my doorstep for at least an hour. Two big burly men, one at the end of his career and one just starting, both covered in snow. As I let them in I saw that another two inches of snow had already fallen and obliterated my footprints that ran up to the alcove that led to my front door. They took my statement, listening intently and asking a few questions here and there to clarify events.

"So someone just picked you up and threw you over?"

"Yes."

"And you didn't get a good look at them."

"I didn't get any look at them. He or she came from behind. And they were wearing a hood."

"Do you have any idea why anyone would want to do that to you?"

I hesitated. "It's not the first time."

They both looked at me expectantly. I told them about the subway and I told them about Ella and Mavis.

"So Ella's a nurse on a psychiatric ward?"

"Yes, that's right."

"And how do you know her?"

The question flustered me and I answered without thinking. "She looks after me."

The two men exchanged a glance.

"You mean you're a patient on the ward?"

"Yes." I caught the younger officer rolling his eyes. This was not going well.

"Why would this Ella want you dead?" he said in a softer, almost condescending voice.

I hesitated again and then I lied, although it wasn't really a lie. "I don't know." Because why would they believe me now?

By the time they left it was 7:00 p.m., and I felt like being with someone. I called my brother, because he was my go-to guy. Ryan was pleased and excited that I was out "on leave" and he invited me for dinner, as I knew he would. I said yes, because suddenly I needed to be with family, whether I could handle it or not. Despite my protestations that I'd take a cab, he came and got me, giving me a bear hug in the front hall of my apartment. I grabbed my coat from the closet, but as I did so something jarred in my mind, but it was gone before I had a chance to think about it.

Ryan lived in a small three-bedroom apartment in the Annex near the University of Toronto. It was as close as the family could get to the Hospital for Sick Children, where Annie's doctor worked.

I played with my little nephew, Davey, for a while, while Annie looked on. She was pale and wan and wore a scarf to cover her bald head. The change in her, from an active curious child to this living ghost of a girl, was devastating. It was also mentally exhausting trying to act as if nothing was wrong — with either her *or* with me — and I finally, reluctantly, had to beg off for a nap before dinner.

When I awoke I could hear the voices of my brother and his wife, Rose, but there was a third familiar voice: my lab tech, Martha. I walked out of the bedroom and down the short hall into the living room. Martha and I hadn't seen each other since before I was hospitalized, and she held me literally at arm's length, scrutinizing my face, which I tried to mould into an affable grin. And then she gave me a bear hug.

"Lookin' pretty good, girl," she said. I expected her to add, "all things considered," but she didn't. I wondered why Duncan wasn't with her. The three of us had solved three different murders over the years, and Martha and Duncan had become a couple. She was looking as Martha as ever. Plump, round, and cheerful, her shoulder-length dark curly hair springing every which way, framing the roundest face you ever saw, but one with delicately pretty features.

We chatted about family and friends and all the other things that good friends talk about, before Ryan called us to dinner. Their dining room was a postage stamp with just enough room for a table and six chairs. There were only four place settings, and I realized that the kids had been put to bed already.

We all sat down to dinner and I was surprised at how easy it was to fall back in with my family and friend, as though nothing had happened to me. To be sitting here talking about new recipes and where to find the best fruits and vegetables, all the minutiae of life that had eluded me for months. But it was all false bonhomie. How could it be otherwise with their Annie's illness hanging over our heads?

"Penny for your thoughts?" I'd fallen silent, and Martha was looking at me uncertainly.

"Surely inflation has brought that up to a toonie?" I answered lightheartedly, not wanting to break the magic by bringing up Annie's illness, the elephant in the room.

She smiled and waited for me to say more.

"Just good to be home," I said rather lamely. We had finished our main course and Rose got up to get dessert.

And that was when Ryan said, "Did that patient ever turn up?" His face was neutral, but his eyes were anything but. Another elephant in the room. I knew what it had taken for him to ask the question and I knew what answer he wanted.

When I didn't say anything Martha asked, "What patient?"

I looked at Ryan and then turned to Martha and told her about Mavis. I saw her glance once at Ryan, but then I had her whole attention. And I didn't stop with what Ryan knew. I told them everything, from Ella to the subway to my flight over the bridge.

"You fell off the bridge? Today?" asked Ryan, the incredulity in his voice obvious.

Martha looked back and forth between us. "You could have been killed," she said. Ryan looked at her and gently shook his head.

"She's your sister and my friend, for cripe's sakes. We have to help her."

Ryan said nothing. He didn't believe me.

"She's my friend."

Words that meant the world to me.

chapter fifteen

It was late by the time I got home. The snow had finally stopped and it was a comfort to see no tracks leading to the alcove that sheltered my front door and my neighbours' from the elements. Martha, who was staying with friends, waited in her car until I flashed my living room lights at her to signal that all was well. I heard the tiny peep of a horn in acknowledgement and watched as she drove around the circle and headed toward the bridge.

I wasn't sleepy. My mind was rushing like the rapids in a river, so I picked up my mail and started going through it all. In the end I must have fallen asleep on the sofa because something woke me, a noise that didn't belong.

I sat bolt upright and listened. It came again, a light tapping sound coming from the bedroom. I looked around for a weapon and my hand closed over a heavy glass paperweight, the kind with dandelion fluff inside. I slowly got up and tiptoed toward the bedroom. I peered around and looked inside, expecting an intruder, a killer,

Ella. Nothing. I went back into the living room. It had sliding glass doors that opened onto my little backyard, which was flanked by my neighbours' yards and carports, and looked into a narrow wooded ravine.

Cautiously I pulled back a curtain and peered out. But I saw nothing, which was a good sign, because there were no footprints. And then the *tap tap* came again and I jumped back. Gathering my wits, I looked out once more and saw a broken tree branch rhythmically hitting the window. It took a while for me to calm down, and longer still to go to bed and fall back asleep. So many images in my mind, so many lost thoughts, so many fears.

When I awoke the next morning I lay in bed awhile looking out the window at the blue sky. Today was yesterday's future where all things were possible, still were possible. A brand-new day. I stretched out and suddenly remembered my fall from the bridge. I sat up and checked myself over, but there had been no noticeable damage from the tree. My coat had been well padded, I guess. Nice if my mind had been padded, too, I thought as I felt the fear steal through it again. I got up to stop it from growing, realizing that in the very act of doing so, I was getting better. I couldn't have got up at all only a short time ago.

I padded into the living room and opened the curtains to let the sun in. But instead, it let in fear. Stark and real.

There were footprints in the snow, coming toward my sliding doors. And there were no footprints going back. I whirled around to look at my front door. The chain was off and as I approached I saw that the bolt was undone. Had I forgotten to lock the door? Or was someone in my apartment with me? The thought was terrifying.

There were lots of places for someone to hide in the condo, and I searched them all, while holding the heavy glass paperweight in one hand. But there was no one but me in my home. Had someone come in through the sliding doors in the night and left by the front door? I did a quick search. Nothing had been stolen and there was no tampering of the lock in the back doors as far as I could see. So where had the footsteps come from? Had I gone to the carport to get something and walked back in my own prints? I couldn't remember. And that was frightening, too. How could I forget?

But why would anyone come into my apartment and leave without taking anything or doing anything? I was just about to get my coat and boots and check the shed, when the phone rang.

It was the police.

"I'm afraid we found no evidence at the bridge," said an officer, who identified himself as Pete Simpson.

"Everything has been covered by the snow."

"What about branches on that tall tree? I know I broke some branches."

"Yes, there were broken branches, but nothing conclusive."

"Nothing conclusive."

"Nothing to corroborate your story."

"Story?" I said.

"Look, Ms O'Callaghan, we spoke with Ms Ella Fraser and she's very worried about you. She wants you back at the hospital as soon as possible."

I felt a shock go through me at the mention of Ella's name. It had never occurred to me that they would talk to her, but of course they had to. I wondered where that left me.

"Look," said Pete again, "we checked out the subway incident, too, and nobody came forward to say you were pushed, and the surveillance tapes are inconclusive. Ella appears to have an alibi, but we'll check it out."

"So what are you saying?"

"That we can't really help you, unless some new evidence comes up. We'll keep your case open for a while," he said.

After we disconnected, I wandered around the apartment for a while, at sixes and sevens, until I finally got my act together and went to get my coat and boots. I pulled my coat off the hanger where I had hung it, and that was when it hit me. How could my coat be in the closet when I had left it at the base of the tree? No, I must have grabbed it, or I would have frozen in that numbing cold. I brushed the memory lapse from my mind and got myself out of my apartment and down to the bus, carrying just a backpack full of my things.

I fervently wished that I could have seen Ella's face when the police told her I'd reported the bridge incident. Surely there would have been a clue at her guilt, might still be. I had one eye out for her as I took the elevator up to the seventh floor and signed myself in at the window of the nurses' station.

As I was walking down the hall toward my room Ella came out of a patient's room and we nearly collided. With her strapping curvaceous body she was certainly big and strong enough to hurl me over the bridge, but to my surprise, she seemed pleased to see me and asked me how my overnight at home had been. She didn't mention the police and appeared genuinely concerned about me. I was confused and held my counsel, while she made encouraging comments about the state of my mental health.

"Going home for a night is the first big step to getting better," she said. I wondered about that. Wasn't the first big step accepting that you were sick in the first place and seeking help?

Our conversation was interrupted by Dr. Osborn, who came out of the same room Ella had been in and took her by the elbow, after a cursory nod to me, and walked down the hallway. It didn't escape my notice the flash of delight in Ella's eyes and the little smile on her face as he took her arm, but whether it was from relief at getting away from me or some other emotion I couldn't say. She was hard to read.

I went into my room and dumped my backpack on my bed. Kit and Lucy were out somewhere and the fourth bed still lay empty, which was a good sign. Maybe it meant that there were no other poor souls out there needing a bed. *Unlikely*, I thought, but for whatever reason, the bed was empty. I lay down on my bed and fell asleep with the sun on my face. When I awoke the sun was long gone. I sat up and rubbed my eyes.

"You sure sleep a lot." The accusatory and cranky voice came from my left. Lucy.

I turned to look at her. She was lounging on her bed, her single pillow propped against the headboard in a vain effort to support her head, which had missed the pillow and was leaning on the headboard.

"Who do you think could have killed Mavis?" I asked point-blank.

"Nothing to say she is dead," countered Lucy aggressively.

"Humour me," I said.

She stared at me for a few moments and I thought she wasn't going to say anything at all. But then she shrugged and said, "Dunno, but she is a bit of a snoop, you know? Always nosing around. Just like you."

"You mean she found out about things that people would rather she didn't?"

Lucy hesitated and then said, "You could say that."

Lucy reached around and tugged at her pillow, as if to signal that the conversation was over. But I had other plans.

"Could she have been blackmailing anyone?"

Lucy narrowed her eyes. "Jesus, lady, you're just like her, maybe worse," she said. "Totally snoopy. Totally inquisitive. Didn't your parents teach you any better?"

"Was she?" I persisted.

Lucy flapped her hands in the air. "Whatever."

I took a stab in the dark. "Was she blackmailing *you?*"

Lucy caught her breath and then pretended it was just the beginning of a deep impatient sigh. But we both knew it wasn't. I just didn't know why. Even though Mavis was wealthy I had my suspicions.

I had a sudden urge for another Tim Hortons coffee, so I put on all my winter gear and, when I saw a lineup at the elevator, I trooped down all seven flights and out into a deeply overcast day. Sort of like my mood. There was a long lineup, but the staff was quick and I soon had my steaming cup of coffee and a double-chocolate doughnut in my hands. I took a table by the window and drank my coffee and watched all the people walk by. Big ones, fat ones, skinny ones, short ones, and decided that the predominant colour for clothing this winter was black.

Suddenly I didn't want to be sitting alone in a coffee shop. It wasn't where I wanted my mind to be. Lonely and alone. I quickly finished my doughnut and scooped up my coffee and left, practically running, hoping to leave my demons behind. I headed east, back toward the hospital, and within seconds could see the front door.

I stopped. Jacques and Lucy were coming out of the door and I really didn't feel like talking to them. I watched with interest as they turned and headed east. What were they doing together? If I had to admit it, maybe I was a little jealous. Lucy was so beautiful and Jacques was a man. Lethal combination. Yet they seemed to be keeping their distance from each other, avoiding any chance physical contact.

So I followed them to University Avenue and then down University to Osgoode Hall, where Toronto lawyers meet for lunch and business. I was standing at the northwest corner of Queen and University, waiting for the light to turn green, when a SUV with tinted windows came out of nowhere, taking a right on a red light. It jumped the curb right at my feet and if a man hadn't grabbed me by the neck of my coat and hauled me out of the way, I would have been a statistic.

I felt slightly sick, but I pulled myself together enough to thank the good Samaritan. I crossed the street and saw Jacques and Lucy enter Osgoode Hall. I was suddenly overcome by another wave of nausea and I sat down on a bench, taking deep breaths and trying to still my nerves. Someone was out to get me. Had they nearly succeeded again? Or was it just a coincidence?

I was pretty sure that Jacques and Lucy were going to the restaurant inside the hall, so I sat there awhile longer, collecting myself. And then I walked up to the doors of Osgoode Hall.

The building was almost two hundred years old, its impressive three stone archways at the front entrance holding up six elegant columns supporting a peaked portico. It reminded me vaguely of a mini Parthenon. I always get a frisson of awe, as if caught in a spine-chilling time warp, whenever I find myself amongst ancient things, with their history spreading out behind me like a taunt, or maybe a lament for all that could have been, but wasn't.

I had been here before. The restaurant is open to the public, where once it was the private domain of lawyers. I had to go through security and empty all my pockets and wait while they eyeballed my stuff. I wondered what the lawyers of the 1840s would have thought of that. Once through, I tried to remember how to get to the restaurant — it had been a while. I walked under vaulted ceilings across mosaic-tiled floors into an ordinary room carpeted in red. I followed the red carpet up a set of stairs and came out into an unobtrusive lobby that held a coat rack and not much else. The main entrance to the restaurant was just off this lobby, and did not advertise itself well. I didn't have a reservation and wasn't really sure what I was going to do to get in unobserved.

I loitered in the lobby for a few minutes, trying to catch glimpses of people in the restaurant. Finally I edged up to the door and looked in. I quickly scanned the room. Jacques was sitting with his back to me at a table for two along the west wall. There was no sign of Lucy. She must have gone to the washroom. A stroke of luck for me. It was early for lunch, so when I asked for a table right behind Jacques's, they were able to accommodate me. I knew the washrooms were in the direction that Jacques was facing so I knew I would be undetected if I sat down before Lucy came back.

I was inches from Jacques, my back to his back, and felt quite proud of myself for being so unobtrusive. I had a moment to relax and I looked around. The cathedral ceiling and the multi-coloured stained-glass windows shaped like archways and candled by the sun, gave the room a feeling of vastness and light. In contrast, the heavy wood panelling and bookshelves with their leather-bound law books that skirted the room, rising ten feet from the floor, gave it a feeling of coziness, which might seem oppressive in the summer, but in winter felt somehow protective. I was just taking in the enormous pendulous multi-light chandelier hanging from the centre of the ceiling and the stanchions between the stained-glass windows, each holding their lights like hands cupping a dove, when I heard sounds behind me that indicated Lucy had returned.

I had to force myself not to turn around and look. When the waiter came I almost panicked, knowing Jacques would recognize my voice. So I dropped my voice an octave and whispered and the poor woman had to bend over me to hear my order. I told her I had laryngitis so she wouldn't think I was a complete idiot. Once she was gone I strained my ears to hear what Jacques and Lucy were saying. Most of it was pretty boring.

Then I heard Jacques say, "Do you believe her?"

"That she saw Mavis dead?"

"Yeah."

"Hard to say," Lucy replied. "Why would the docs cover it up? We're all adults. We know people die."

"Yeah, but they usually don't die in a psychiatric hospital. We're supposed to be safe there. Protected."

"Personally I believe the authorities when they say she's been moved to another floor."

There was a silence and then Lucy said, "Maybe she just thought Mavis was dead, you know, mistook death for a deep sleep."

"That's not what she says. What's wrong with her, anyway? Why is she in hospital?" said Jacques.

"Don't know and that may be because they don't know yet. Sometimes a diagnosis can be difficult and because she's so —"

There was a loud guffaw and four very noisy people descended on the table to my left and proceeded to drown out Lucy and Jacques. It was just as well, for I was unnerved. I did not like it one bit that people were talking about my illness. It made me feel powerless, and the fact that it was Jacques doing the asking made things complicated. Did he ask because he cared about me, or did he ask because he thought I was crazy and wanted corroboration, so that he could run as far away from me as he could, as fast as he could? But then, he did say more than once that he believed me. I had to stop second-guessing myself.

I couldn't resist the urge to turn around and watch them when they left by the other entrance to the restaurant. And wished I hadn't. Jacques was giving Lucy a one-armed hug. She was looking at him, laughing. It made me wonder. And I think the little shiver I felt was another pang of jealousy. Was he just another womanizer?

Another ladies' man? I tried to put that out of my mind and I found that I was suddenly ravenous. I hadn't eaten for a while and I ate my now cold club sandwich, which was still pretty good. I debated asking for a glass of wine, but it wasn't as much fun drinking alone. Besides, wine would interfere with my meds.

Out of curiosity I glanced over at Jacques and Lucy's table to see if they'd had wine. I don't know why I cared so much about Jacques's resolve to stop drinking, but I was relieved to see there was no wineglass in front of his seat, only one in front of Lucy's. I sat and listened to the voices drifting over my head for a long time before I finally got up and went back to the hospital. I felt so normal that it seemed kind of ridiculous for me to go back at all, but Ryan and Martha would be frantic if I didn't, so I did.

I fell asleep on my bed with my winter coat still on and awoke sweating. I peeled off my coat and saw that Kit was lying curled up on her bed with her back to me. We all did that, turning away from the world, to get some privacy. Human nature, I guess.

I wandered out into the hall. It was still too early for dinner, but I was really thirsty, so I went to the common room to get some juice. I thought I was the only one there until I heard someone clear his throat and I turned to see the back of Jacques's blond head, the rest of him hidden by the sofa. I picked up a juice container and went around the sofa so that he could see me. His eyes were shut and his face was relaxed as if he was asleep. He looked sad and vulnerable and I turned to go.

"Everything okay?" came his voice.

I turned back, and hesitated. Despite the unwritten code in the ward that you don't ask people how they are, he always seemed to be asking me.

"I could ask the same of you," I said as he opened his eyes. I don't know why, but I half expected them to be dim and unfocused, but they were sharp and clear.

"I'm fine," he said. "Nobody's trying to kill me." He said it as a joke, but then he saw my face and said, "What's wrong?"

"They tried again."

Jacques sat upright, his attention one hundred percent on me. "What happened?" he asked, his voice insistent and urgent.

I sat down beside him and he moved close enough to me that our legs were touching. I suddenly thought about Lucy and wondered if I should move away from him, but I couldn't. The warmth of his leg felt too good. Instead of answering his question, I jerked my attention back to his face and said, "I saw you with Lucy."

I was expecting him to look guilty, but he didn't. In fact, he laughed and said, "She's a handful, that one. But I'm more interested in you. Tell me what happened."

I wanted to believe him and his interest seemed genuine. So I told him about the bridge and my descent through the tree and the hard slog through the snow as my would-be killer zeroed in on me. I didn't mention the near miss with the car today, because, despite my fears, it may well have been an accident. I didn't want Jacques to think I was paranoid.

"Did you see anyone before you went over the bridge?"

I shook my head. "My attacker came from behind. I never got a good look."

"Did you feel anything, taste anything, hear anything, smell anything that might help? Maybe perfume?"

I thought back to the bridge. There was nothing to feel except the strength of the arms that grabbed me. The snow had muffled everything and my attacker had said nothing. And there had been no smell, no perfume, no deodorant, not surprising given the bitter cold and the layers of clothing.

"Nothing," I said, and then asked, "Was Ella on duty yesterday evening?"

He reached over and took my hand in his. I felt a little rattled by the warmth of his hand and the fact that mine had completely disappeared in his. He cocked his head and seemed to think for a moment. "Damn it. I can't remember," he said finally. "I wasn't feeling so well, so I went to bed."

That changed the subject for awhile, until I said, "I called the police."

"Good. What did they say?"

"Inconclusive."

"Just what they said about the subway," said Jacques.

"How did you know that?" I asked.

"Word gets around." He looked at me and shrugged. I was about to tell him about the footprints in the snow when he said bitterly, "Some bodyguard I am."

"You may have offered to be my bodyguard, but that only works while I'm on the floor."

"And whoever wants to kill you only tries when you're off the floor. Strange, that," he said, and added softly, his eyes amused, "Maybe I should follow you home."

chapter sixteen

Jacques confused me. He seemed genuinely interested in my problems, but maybe he was only interested in me. Maybe he *was* a hustler, a ladies' man out for the conquest. I had no way of knowing and I found that I cared. He attracted me, not just intellectually but physically, but I felt as though I was standing on quicksand with him.

I fell asleep dreaming about his smile and what it meant when it was aimed my way, but the dreams turned to nightmares and I awoke suddenly in the night in a panic. A plaintive wail, so desolate and disconsolate as to defy even imagination, ripped through the hallways, echoing upon itself in a dreadful reminder that a mind feels pain, too. I lay in bed shivering, but the cries went on and on, until finally subsiding into sobs of despair.

"Jesus, what was that?" said Lucy.

"New inmate," said Kit, the choice of word leaving no doubt how she felt about the place.

"That's how Mavis came in, like a fucking banshee," said Lucy.

"Suicidal, until she had an ECT," said Kit.

There was a long pause and then I asked, "Did the ECT help her?"

"Wiped out her memory the first time," said Kit. "She was like a lost little child. Couldn't remember anything and then as her memories came back she swore she'd never have another one, no matter how much it helped her. She didn't want to forget her life. Lucky her. She had a life worth remembering."

Silence wrapped itself around that little thought until I said, "But she had another one."

"Yeah," said Kit. "That was really weird, but after she talked to Bradley one day, she decided to go ahead and try it again." Bradley, the other Scientologist, with the long black hair and the straggley beard.

"What did Bradley say to her?"

"No idea, but he somehow managed to calm her down. She hated ECT."

"And then she died?"

Kit just stared at me.

"Jesus, you two. Can't a person get any sleep around here?" said Lucy.

After that I tossed and turned for hours, those cries of torment seared on my mind.

When I got up the next morning and went for breakfast I passed the suicide room, the name given to the room immediately across from the nursing station. The wall on the corridor side was all glass, so the nurses could see the patient at all times. It also meant that we could see the patient, too, and as I passed, I looked in and saw a hefty woman lying on the bed, her back to our peering eyes, curled up in the fetal position underneath a thin blanket. She was lying there motionless and her curly, dark, shoulder-length hair spilled out over the bed covers. Talk about having no privacy. Whoever it was looked as though she were asleep, but she could just as easily have been wide awake, staring with unseeing eyes at the blank wall, lost in the terror of a mind torn to shreds by mental illness.

In the cafeteria I picked up my tray and helped myself to some pancakes and a juice, while simultaneously looking to see where I might sit. As usual Bradley was at a table all by himself, Leo hadn't arrived yet, and Lucy, Kit, Austin, and Jacques were sitting at a table for six. I went and sat right across the table from Jacques and beside Austin, who hunched over his food as soon as I arrived, as if afraid I'd take it.

"She tried to jump off a bridge," said Lucy suddenly as she flicked her head in the direction of the suicide room.

"How do you know that?" asked Jacques.

Lucy shrugged. "She's on suicide watch." As if that answered his question.

"What does that mean?" I asked.

"What do you think it means? Just what it says," snapped Lucy. "They'll just keep an eye on her until the meds kick in and then she'll be out with the rest of us."

"How long does that usually take?"

"Not long. The meds usually work to some extent or other and the docs don't want us to linger here for very long," said Lucy. "Long stays are discouraged, and so they fill us with meds, stabilize us, and discharge us before we're ready. It's not their fault. It's too expensive to do more. That's one of the reasons why the streets are full of mentally ill people."

We ate in silence for a while and then I said, "So Mavis was suicidal, was she?"

"Aren't we all?' said Austin. "Comes with the territory. If life is hopeless and you are helpless to do anything about it, what else is there?"

"Mavis came in on an overdose," said Kit, "and on the day she died she was scared shitless, almost as if she knew."

"Knew what?" said Lucy.

"Knew that she would either get better or get worse."

"Duh," said Lucy.

I quickly changed the subject.

"How do you know that woman tried to jump off a bridge?" I asked, repeating Jacques's query and tilting my head in the direction of the suicide room.

Lucy eyed me like I was some sort of pinned insect.

"Ever heard of the nurses' station? You should try hanging out by their door sometime. Lots of juicy stuff." I looked at her and wondered if she knew I had done just that. Then I looked at Jacques and he winked at me.

"So what about the scarf?" I asked, hoping to startle an answer out of someone by bringing it up out of the blue. If you don't ask the questions you don't get the answers. And maybe the nurses had been talking.

"Nothing, just that they said it was wound around her neck, but then, you knew that already," said Lucy. Austin made a noise as if he had been startled, and I looked over at him and caught his eye. He looked away hastily and I wondered what had bothered him.

"You mean, they said it strangled her?" I asked.

"Why would they say that? She isn't dead."

I wasn't listening to Lucy anymore. My mind had swung back to the morgue, to Mavis's body. The image of the tiny silver cross was clear in my head. There had been no marks on her smooth white neck to indicate that she had been strangled by a scarf.

After I'd eaten I took my dirty tray to the kitchen area, and on my way back I passed Bradley's table. He was hunched over, writing something in a notebook and I noticed that he had dropped a piece of paper on the floor. I stooped to pick it up and held it out to him. He pretended not to see me, so I put it on his table and said, "You a writer?"

His pen stopped moving and his whole body stilled as he digested my question. I thought he wasn't going to answer, but suddenly he blurted, "Writing is a calling. It's something I have to do. It consumes me."

"Is that a good thing?" I asked, because it actually sounded like a burden.

"It's just a thing. My thing. It can be good and it can be bad and it can be awesome, but it belongs to me and nobody has a right to take it away from me."

"Who would take it away from you?"

He looked at me, gauging something, as if wondering if he could trust me.

"ECT."

I mentally whistled, not sure what to say.

"You've had ECT?" I asked.

"No," he said. "But my doctors tell me it will help me."

"But you don't think it will?"

"I'm afraid it will hurt my writing, and I couldn't bear that," he said.

"You seem to have convinced Mavis to try again," I said, taking a chance.

He looked up at me so abruptly that I almost jumped back. But he said nothing for a while, neither confirming nor denying, as if Mavis's name had never come up.

"Do you know Ernest Hemingway?" he finally asked.

I nodded politely.

"He killed himself because he said ECT had ruined his career by taking away his memory. Do you know what he said?"

I shook my head.

"He said, and I quote, 'Well, what is the sense of ruining my head and erasing my memory, which is my capital, and putting me out of business? It was a brilliant cure but we lost the patient.'"

I wasn't sure what to say to that, either.

"He's not alone, you know. Lots of people with mental illness fear losing their ability to write or create. It seems so unfair to be thrown a choice: more madness or lose the only thing you value."

"But Dr. Osborn says ECT really does help some people. The memory loss is temporary."

"For most people," Bradley said. "Osborn your doctor?"

He asked this in a way that made me feel funny, so I didn't answer him. Instead I said, "Did you write the poem outside the nursing station?"

He refused to look at me, but there was an almost imperceptible nod of his head and he went back to scribbling in his book.

"I liked it," I said, but he was lost to his writing. Something didn't quite jibe about his writing, or about him, or both, but I couldn't put my finger on it.

I left him then and went back to my room, where I fell asleep. When I awoke I tried to decide whether to go to the spirituality group or cognitive behavioural therapy. I was torn. They were both interesting in their own right, but in the end I opted for the spirituality group because it was less focused and more free flow. As before, the lights had been dimmed around a circle of chairs, though the whiff of incense wasn't quite as strong this time. Why is it that dim light, the stuff of demons and twilight, can soothe a mind, as well as terrify it? There was no doubt that it was soothing, but so many of my nightmares took place in twilit places of terror. So why was it soothing? Why did cocooning in soft, low light make us feel safe, when in the hands of horror-movie directors it was anything but?

Austin was already there, head down, tapping his foot to a beat all his own — it certainly wasn't to the music that was playing. He didn't look up and so I gave him his privacy and took a seat across from him. The minister came in and gave me a kind smile that was a little bit sad. I wondered yet again what it must be like to try to help the mentally injured.

Others began to trickle in. Lucy, Leo, then Bradley and Austin, and two other patients I didn't know, other than seeing them in the hall. Jacques shuffled in and took a seat beside Lucy. Kit came sidling through the door as if it would bite her. She came and sat down beside me, and

Lucy smiled at her, the same sad smile that the minister had given to me. The kind of smile that said, everything is okay but everything isn't, and maybe it will be okay one day, and maybe it won't.

The minister went and closed the door and then came back to the circle and sat down. She asked if anyone had anything to say to start the group off. Everybody's eyes flickered all over the place, but no one said anything. She let the silence grow. I could hear Kit breathing and Jacques's stomach rumbling. Into the silence Austin said, "Sometimes I don't know what is real and what is an hallucination."

He stared at the minister, daring her to say something. When she didn't he said, "I keep seeing a woman. She always wears a silk sari that swirls around her in a fluid graceful motion. She is not Indian, but she has long dark hair and dark brown eyes, and she is stunningly beautiful. She holds me under her spell. She never tells me what I should do. She tells me what I shouldn't have done. I know she is not real, because my friends have told me they can't see her, but she is real to me. If she let me, I would hug her, but she won't. And I want to, so much, but she always finds fault with me and keeps me at a distance."

He looked around the room at all of us in turn and said, "Each of you has your own little hell. Mine is knowing that there are alien entities out to get me, and my beautiful woman can't help me. I know this because they communicate with me through my cellphone. And she makes me very anxious by telling me they will get me. But she never says how I can escape."

I wondered what the minister was going to say to all this. I knew enough to know that she would have been coached to not support the delusions and hallucinations, but to support the emotions that surrounded them. I had read that somewhere in a book when I was trying to diagnose myself.

"That must be very disturbing for you," she said to Austin.

His mouth fell open and he laughed, and so did Bradley. They played off each other, their laughter cold and sterile and full of hopelessness.

When Austin finally composed himself he said to the minister, "You're good at understatement, aren't you?" He snorted and then added, "Have you any idea of the fear and the terror associated with knowing alien creatures are stalking you? It tears at your guts, strangles your mind, and suffocates your heart. What else is left? It doesn't matter one whit that *you* don't think it's real — and I know you don't because I have seen it in your eyes, everybody's eyes, in fact — because it is real to me and that's all that counts. It's as real as all of us sitting here, including my brown-eyed lady." He looked pointedly at the empty chair beside me and we all followed his gaze.

"I think maybe I shouldn't have come." The voice came from my right. Leo. He was trembling and gripping his knees hard with his bony hands.

"Are you all right?" asked the minister with some concern.

"I know that if I believed that aliens were out to kill me, I'd have a panic attack before they could even touch me."

"But they aren't," said the minister in a firm tone.

Leo ignored her and looked at Austin. "I would never survive your illness. I'd have a panic attack at the first hallucination. It would kidnap my mind, hold it hostage. And I don't always need a trigger. The anxiety is paralyzing, physically and emotionally. I can't think rationally. I can go from being told my girlfriend is going to be late for dinner to thinking, *Why is she going to be late?* to, *Oh, no! Is she meeting someone else?* to, *Oh, my God, is she cheating on me?* to, *I don't want to lose her and I have to stop her at any cost!*"

He stopped suddenly, a look of fear creasing his face. No one spoke, but everyone was thinking about what Leo had said. I couldn't help but wonder if such intense anxiety could drive a person to do something violent, out of sheer desperation to get rid of the anxiety.

"At any cost," repeated Jacques. "Sometimes I think I would do anything to get a drink." There was a long silence as everyone swung their attention from Leo to Jacques.

"But you've been sober for how long?" asked the minister finally.

"Two weeks, forty days, what does it matter? It is its own agony. It festers like an open wound in my mind." He scanned all our faces and said, "Have any of you ever been addicted to anything?"

I saw Austin squirm and Bradley crossed his arms, hugging his chest. We weren't supposed to ask questions like that.

"If you have then you know it is a physical force that takes over your body and your mind. You think, *I'll just have one drink. Can't hurt.* Oh, but it can and it does. Because it feels so good to have a drink, to let all your cares evaporate with the fumes of the liquor or whatever your poison is."

The minister tried to interject but Jacques talked over her. "And the cure isn't to cut back. It's total abstinence. The only thing close to it that everybody might understand is having to give up sex forever, even masturbation."

"You have supports that can help you," said the minister quickly. "I know you don't believe in God, but I'd be happy to write up the twelve steps for you with all references to God deleted. It would be a start."

Jacques smiled a grimacing sort of smile at her and I thought about his lonely fight with alcohol and whether he really did have family and friends to support him. And I found I cared. I cared very much.

When the class ended I left quickly. I didn't want to talk to anyone, especially Jacques. I was feeling too unsure of myself. Unfortunately, to get to my room I had to pass the suicide room. There was no other way. And like people at a train wreck, I was unable to walk by without looking.

She was out of bed, her back to me, and I had a sudden sense of unease as I watched her round shape standing there forlornly. As if sensing my eyes on her, she slowly turned around, and I felt totally discombobulated when she brought a finger to her lips and pursed them in the universal signal to keep quiet.

It was a face I knew well. It was Martha's.

chapter seventeen

I was equal parts confused, alarmed, and angry. What the hell was Martha doing here? Did she really try to commit suicide? Martha? No chance. Not a happier woman existed in all the world. So why was she here, then? All sorts of scenarios swirled around in my mind and I was frantic for an answer, but brought up short by her silent request to keep quiet. So I knew I couldn't just barge into her room. The nurses would want to know why and haul me out of there.

I loitered in the hall, knowing that Martha would have to go to the washroom sometime. I began to pace the hall and noticed that where Bradley's poem had been there was a new notice, with no blank space for graffiti. Although Bradley's poem was a cut above graffiti, I thought. *God's disgrace*, he'd written. Why? For what purpose? And then it occurred to me what hadn't seemed right when I was talking to Bradley. Why would a devout Scientologist write a poem about God's disgrace? But the thought was chased from my mind because suddenly Martha was there, shuffling toward me, head down, oozing dejection. I'd never seen Martha like that and it scared me.

She passed me by without seeming to notice me, and I turned and followed her into the washroom. I peered under the stalls to see if anyone was there, but they were all empty.

Choosing my words carefully, I said, "What's happening?"

She turned to face me and I saw that her eyes were swollen, and her face portrayed pure misery.

"Martha! What's happening?" I asked again, in great alarm.

And then she smiled — and had the decency to look guilty about it. "I thought you could use some help and it was the only thing I could think of to do," she said.

I stood there with my jaw hanging loose and wondered if her deception was a delusion.

"You said someone was trying to kill you," she said. "I'm just watching your back."

I was horrified and touched at the same time, but the horror got the better of me. "Jesus, Martha, you can't go impersonating a suicide. What if someone else really needs the bed?"

"You told me yourself that you've had an empty bed since that woman died."

"Mavis."

"Yeah, Mavis."

"That was you? The screaming and moaning?"

"Yeah."

"Where did you ever learn to act like that?" I asked.

"From watching you," she said.

God, had it been that obvious over the years? Her words hit me like a kick in the gut, because I had always believed that I had hidden my pain so well. I had to hand it to Martha. She was a good actor. I couldn't understand why she was working for me and not on stage somewhere. "Did you really try to jump off a bridge?" I asked, afraid of the answer.

"Governor's Bridge. There seemed to be a certain, I don't know, synchronicity with you."

"And you made the police talk you down?" I asked, thinking about all the people she must have scared half to death. I couldn't believe she'd done it.

"Yeah," she said. "I had to do it. I just had to. I couldn't leave you alone in this."

I was too emotionally exhausted to have it out with her. She was here now and I marvelled at the strength of her friendship, that she did this for me.

"Martha, you can't stay, you know that," was all I could manage.

She avoided looking at me and said, "Maybe it's not all an act, Cordi."

I must have looked pretty incredulous because she said, "All right, but I had to come and help."

I knew her behaviour was wrong, but I suddenly really needed a friend to lean on. I was about to give her a hug when Kit came into the room and stared at us before going into a cubicle. Martha silently saluted me and went into another cubicle and I left to nurse my thoughts.

I decided to go swimming. There was a notice on the bulletin board that said we could use the facilities of a place nearby and I needed some exercise. Anything to distract me from myself. I signed myself out and almost signed myself back in again when I discovered how cold and windy and snowy it was outside. But I forced myself to walk the block to the community centre. I had a bit of difficulty finding the changing rooms because, while the pool was on the first floor, the changing rooms were in the basement. So I went down to the grungy school-locker-room-style change rooms to change and then had to traipse up eighteen stairs to the pool area. One wall of the pool was floor-to-ceiling windows and the light that flowed into the pool danced with the waves in undulating ripples.

I scanned the pool to see which of the cordoned-off lanes was the least congested for doing laps and found myself looking at Jacques as he pulled himself expertly out of the pool, the muscles in his arms and chest rippling and taut like an athlete in his prime. I wondered how on earth he could look like that and be a depressive alcoholic smoker. Was it even possible for someone who is depressed to look after themselves that well? But there he was, a regular blond giant of an Adonis. Without noticing me, he walked over to the side of the pool and picked up his towel, and I felt like a voyeur with a galloping heart. Who was this man?

Eventually he noticed me, probably because I slipped and fell and felt like a total idiot. He hurried over and helped me up. I felt odd standing there, with him half-naked and me half-naked, and I was at a loss for words. Fortunately he wasn't.

"Nice suit," he said, his eyes travelling slowly down my black-and-red one-piece and up again. I felt like saying, "Nice abs," in return because who says, "Nice swim trunks," to a man? Instead, I hugged myself and smiled at him, wishing we were somewhere else.

"Aren't you taking a chance leaving the floor?" he asked. "I would have escorted you here if you'd told me."

When I'd decided to go swimming, all I had thought about was getting there and getting into the pool and swimming some mind-numbing laps. I had actually forgotten about the danger to my life. Was my apparent poor memory because of the ECT I'd had?

"I've been thinking about that," I lied. "If I'm only in danger when off the floor, but I am in danger because of something on the floor, what does it mean?"

"Whoever it is does not, it would appear, want to draw attention to the floor. Mavis is the key. It keeps coming down to why she died and how she died being the questions we need to answer."

"Well, one thing I know for sure," I said. "The red scarf was not the murder weapon."

Jacques eyed me with interest. "How so?"

"When I saw her in the morgue the scarf was gone and her neck was smooth and white. No marks."

Jacques towelled his head and said, "Interesting. So how did she die?"

"She could have been smothered, like Austin said."

"Or given an overdose or a needle full of air. Any number of ways to die prematurely in a hospital."

"How can we ever know?" I asked.

"We keep snooping," he said, which was a peculiar thing to say, I thought, since I seemed to be the only one doing the snooping. It suddenly occurred to me that he hadn't actually told me one new thing to help with the investigation. And yet he had been the one to egg me on. Curious.

After he left I slipped into the pool. The monotony of swimming lengths was somehow relaxing, almost like meditation, with the altered sense of sound, the rhythmic breathing, the going nowhere with a purpose, which was precisely what I felt I was doing. Going nowhere with a purpose. I was really disturbed by Martha's appearance on the scene and at a loss as to how to handle it. I had wanted to tell Jacques, but held back because Martha wanted to be incognito.

When I finished my laps I floated on my back in the deep end for a while; everybody had left and there was no one here but me. I had the pool to myself. Then I heard the muffled sound of a door shutting and I treaded water and looked around. And froze.

Ella was walking toward me, her large voluptuous body crammed into a tiny piece of real estate. She was staring right at me and I looked around quickly again to see if anyone else was around. No one. I looked back at her as I treaded water, realizing how easy it would be for her to overpower and drown me right here in the pool. I imagined myself struggling for air, her strong arms holding my head underwater, my legs and arms thrashing uselessly as my world slowly went black.

But Ella surprised me and raised her hand in a little salute as she slipped into a lane and took off with an impressive crawl. I got out of the pool quickly and went down to the changing room, wondering why Ella hadn't taken advantage of the situation. It would have been risky, but it could have been done.

I pulled on my clothes and trudged back to the hospital through the drifting snow and the winter winds.

I really didn't feel like going back. Being in the hospital was such a pointed admission that I was sick, and I didn't feel sick anymore, just a little confused by how everyone was treating me, as if I *was* still sick. I was almost at the main doors of the hospital when someone I recognized came out.

Despite the cold and the snow he wasn't wearing a hat, and as he stepped outside he drew his hood over his head. Thinning hair. Austin.

I decided it would be more interesting to follow him than to go back to my room. He headed west and then south on Spadina, and then west again into Kensington Market. He seemed to be on a mission and he did not deviate from it, not even to loiter a little in front of a shop window. He kept his head down and walked with short fast steps, somehow avoiding everyone in his path. When he stopped suddenly at the intersection of Augusta and Nassau I had to scramble for cover to avoid being seen, although since I was covered head to toe in winter clothing I probably didn't have to worry.

I stood and looked at a pair of bright-pink rubber boots hanging in the window of a small shop, while keeping him in my peripheral vision. Twice he crossed the street, and twice he came back, and as I watched, a person all dressed in black, face hidden by a scarf, brushed by Austin and handed him a small bag. Austin appeared to give him something in return and the two parted company after what seemed like a choreographed dance, one that had been performed many times before.

chapter eighteen

I was frozen by the time I got back to the hospital and I crawled into bed and fell into a long deep and troubled sleep. Troubled as it was, sleep was my saviour, and the saviour of the mentally ill everywhere. Sleep dulled the pain the way nothing else could, because when you are in a dreamless sleep nothing bad can touch you. That I awoke feeling unrefreshed and groggy did not diminish sleep's ability to soften life's terrors — at least when the nightmares didn't come.

I noticed that Mavis's bed had been used and there was a sweater I recognized dumped on top of the sheets. Martha was to be our new roommate. How weird and unnerving was that? I knew I should force her to leave, but I didn't have the emotional strength to do it. I looked at my watch and realized that it was suppertime and I was actually hungry. I was feeling very antisocial, and so once I had got my food, I took a table far from everyone. Martha nodded at me and I nodded back. She was sitting beside Jacques, who appeared to be trying to get her to smile. Inexplicably I felt jealous as I watched Martha and Mr. Adonis Jacques connecting in some way. Head down, I ate and returned to my room and went back to bed. I must have dozed off because I awoke with a start when I heard a kerfuffle as my roommates came to bed. Then there was a long silence.

I had my back to them and the covers pulled up over my head when Kit said, "Have you met our new roomie yet?"

There was no answer from Lucy, although maybe she nodded or shook her head.

"They've released her from the suicide room. Did you see how she just sat there all alone until Jacques moved in?"

"Was he trying to hustle her?"

"Dunno. She's kind of old for him, fat too, but she kind of spent the evening in a daze."

"Wouldn't you, too, if you'd just tried to off yourself and failed?"

Another silence fell, and then I heard someone else shuffle into the room. No doubt Martha.

"Did you really try to jump off a bridge?" asked Lucy.

"What's it to you?" Martha snapped.

"Just that women don't usually jump. They take pills or something. Men jump off bridges, but then, you weren't successful, were you?"

I held my breath. How was she going to respond to that?

"You treat all your roommates like this?"

Silence.

"Is that why your last roommate died?" Martha asked. "You badgered her to death, made her feel two inches tall, taunted her?"

Martha was overdoing it.

"How the hell do you know anything about our last roommate?" said Lucy. "You've only been here a day. And besides, she's not dead. Why would you think she was?"

"I saw her lying there," said Kit out of the blue, and Lucy jumped in and changed the subject back to Martha. I wondered about that. What had Kit meant?

"What's it like to stand on a bridge and contemplate a swan dive?" Lucy said.

"What do you think it's like?" said Martha angrily. "There isn't a single thing worth living for. Your mind is numb, dead, hopelessly unalive. There's nothing you want to do, say, change. All you feel is pain, and you just want the pain to stop. And I couldn't even be successful at that."

Wow, I thought. *Where did that come from?*

"So why didn't you jump?"

I was waiting for Martha to be angry with Lucy again, but she surprised me by saying, "The policewoman said there was always help, always a way out of the pain I was in. That life was precious and we only get one chance at it. I guess I didn't want to die because I believed her and here I am now, full of meds. I still feel really shitty, but I'm glad I'm not dead."

She said the last part in a whisper that made me very uneasy and no one said anything after that.

The next morning after breakfast I signalled to Martha to follow me. We went down to the end of the hall where there was little or no traffic and I was about to speak when she beat me to it.

"There's something fishy about Jacques," she said, and I felt the strong urge to defend him, even though I didn't know his crime. Turns out neither did she.

"He's just not … right," said Martha.

"Well, yeah," I said sarcastically. "He's here because he's an alcoholic, he smokes, and he's depressed."

"Just seems like he's acting, that's all," she said. And all my misgivings about Jacques came to the fore. "I mean, how many alcoholic smokers do you know that are in such great physical shape?"

She was right. As well as seeing his buff body at the pool, I remembered walking up the stairs with him and he hadn't broken a sweat. And he'd hesitated when I had asked him what his poison was. What alcoholic doesn't know his favourite drink? And he was inordinately interested in helping me find Mavis's murderer. I couldn't put that down to pure interest in me, much as I would have liked to. Any beliefs on that score had been shattered when I saw him with Lucy and then with Martha. Well, maybe not "shattered" exactly. Maybe just slightly cracked. And also, he'd known about the subway. Maybe he hadn't overheard it at the nurses' station.

"What are you saying?" I asked.

"That he isn't who he says he is. That he's acting and it's not a seamless performance."

"But you can't have spent more than ten minutes with him. How the hell could you know so fast?" I was pissed off, but it may have been because I had a sneaking suspicion that she was right.

"I can always spot a bad actor."

"Why would he be acting?" I asked, but I knew she had hit on something.

"You tell me."

Reluctantly I told her then about my misgivings and the feeling I had that he was hiding something.

"Maybe he murdered Mavis and just wants to keep you close in case you break the case and then he'll silence you before you can tell anyone."

"But why would he murder Mavis?"

"I don't know. Maybe it was a lovers' quarrel? Or maybe he's an assassin and she was stealing secrets." Martha was going overboard again.

I thought back with a chill to the attempts on my life.

"So what you're saying is if he murdered Mavis, that would mean he's the one who has been trying to kill me."

"Is that so far-fetched?"

Not completely far-fetched. But it was bad. I liked Jacques. I liked him very much.

"But I overheard Ella in the morgue saying I knew too much," I said. "I was so sure it was her."

"Maybe you misheard," she said, echoing my thoughts. "You were, after all, in a morgue drawer." Martha had a way with words.

"It's not just Jacques. Some of the others are behaving weirdly," I said. And I told her about Austin and Kensington Market.

"Wow," said Martha. "Do you think he was buying drugs?"

"He was doing something that required stealth, because the transaction was furtive. Can you imagine if it was drugs?"

"What do you mean?"

"He's schizophrenic," I said. "The last thing a schizophrenic needs is to be on some wild drug-induced high. It may be why he's not getting better. I don't know how long he's been on the floor, but he was here when I arrived and is definitely having a hard time. His meds don't seem to be working all that well."

"What if Mavis found out?" asked Martha.

"He'd have been screwed. They might have kicked him off the floor, sent him to some other less lenient facility, not to mention the police would get involved."

"Assuming Mavis told him," said Martha.

"You think she forced his hand?"

"To murder her? I suppose it's possible, especially if he had her mixed up in some kind of delusion."

"Or maybe she was blackmailing him," I said, "if he's wealthy. But then, Mavis was wealthy, so why would she resort to blackmail? Except maybe she wasn't so wealthy anymore. Maybe she gave it all to the Church of Scientology."

We thought about that for a while and then I said, "Kit said something weird last night when we were all in our room."

"I knew you were awake. I just knew it."

"Anyway, remember when she said, 'I saw her lying there'? What did she mean by that? She was hiding something that Lucy didn't want me to know."

"Could she have been talking about Mavis?"

"You mean, she actually saw her dead, but won't say?" I raised my eyebrows. "And Lucy was protecting her?"

"Have they done anything else suspicious?" asked Martha.

"Well, yeah. I caught them embracing the other day."

"What of it? Women hug all the time."

"What if it's more than that?" I said.

"Women do that all the time, too."

Martha seemed about to say more when Lucy came out of our room and called to us to come quickly. I glanced at Martha and the two of us hurried back to our room. I'm not sure what I was expecting to find — something horrible for sure, such as a dead Kit — but instead Kit was standing motionless by the window, focused on something on the window ledge.

It was the black squirrel, sitting there and staring back at her, as if taunting us all with its odd reality. *Was he our literal version of Churchill's black dog?* I wondered.

I was glad that so many people had seen the black squirrel, which I didn't just imagine that Ella had seen. She really had. So had I. I felt really strong and decided to go to CBT class. I was a little late and ended up interrupting Leo as he was talking about his panic attacks again, but this time he was talking specifics and not hypotheticals.

"They just seem to come out of nowhere, but sometimes my panic attacks are triggered by people saying or doing something."

The instructor was a new man, slim, in his early thirties, with either a heavy beard shadow or a beard that was just growing in. Apparently the older instructor was sick. He motioned me to a seat and said, "Would you like to give us an example?" Leo hesitated while I sat down between Jacques and Lucy and across from Leo and Bradley.

"Well," said Leo, "there is this woman I knew. I really liked her and I wanted to send her flowers and ask her out. But I was afraid."

"Why? What thought comes to mind?"

"What if she refused?"

"You thought something bad would happen?"

"It'd mean she didn't like me, that she never would."

"And how did that make you feel?"

"Helpless. Sad. Frustrated. Angry." The instructor wrote everything down on the huge pad of paper propped up on an easel.

"What would your automatic first thought be if she refused?"

"That I'm a loser. No good. That she'll never want me. She wasn't exactly an amazing catch and it makes me angry that I'm not even good enough for someone like her."

Leo had suddenly become belligerent and I started listening more carefully.

The instructor wrote it all down and then said, "What would your hot thought be?"

"That she isn't interested in me. That no one will ever love me. That I'll die alone." Leo looked down at his feet. I could see the sweat breaking out on his forehead and he was wringing his hands.

"And that would trigger a panic attack."

"Yeah, sometimes," Leo muttered.

I stared at Leo. An idea began to form in my mind.

"Are you okay to go on, Leo?" asked the instructor.

Leo looked up and nodded.

"Those are a lot of hot thoughts," the instructor said. "Let's concentrate on one. What is your evidence that she wasn't interested in you?"

Leo moaned.

"Did you ask her out?"

Leo nodded his head.

"And how did that go?"

"We were a couple for a while."

The instructor hesitated and then said, "That sounds all good. Why were you worried? Were you losing her?"

Leo nodded, a look of misery spreading over his face.

"Okay. So what is the evidence against your hot thought that she wasn't interested in you anymore?"

Leo squirmed in his seat and said nothing.

"Okay, then," said the instructor finally, "what would be a balanced response to your hot thought?"

Leo sat mute and so did the instructor. Leo won again.

"Maybe it's not that she wasn't interested in you, but that she was busy at work or she had indigestion the times you were together."

Leo cleared his throat. I could see him processing the information. At last he said, "You mean she likes me, but can't be with me because she's got indigestion?"

I looked at the instructor, wondering how he would get out of this mess. He took his time answering, and I wondered if he was new at this.

"Look at the bigger picture," he said. "You don't know what other people are thinking and so it's never a good idea to tie your sense of self-worth to someone else. They may be thinking good things about you and you think they're thinking bad things. Think of all the anxiety that can cause, and maybe for no good reason. In your case her reasons for appearing uninterested are unknown, but you decided they were bad when they might just as easily have been good. You don't want to trigger a panic attack on a whim."

Leo looked confused and chagrined all at the same time.

"But May —"

He stopped abruptly, but the damage was done. I knew then. But it was Austin who suddenly said, with an incredulous laugh, "Holy shit. You're doing Mavis."

Leo swung his head so quickly around to Austin that whiplash came to my mind.

"You don't 'do' your girlfriend," Leo said, the disgust evident in his words. He lowered his voice and said again, "You don't 'do' your girlfriend. That's just rude."

I had a moment of doubt. Was he really talking about Mavis? But then I remembered Ella telling me that Leo didn't like to talk about Mavis because it upset him. Enough to sometimes trigger panic attacks. And at the spirituality class with the minister, he'd talked about a panic attack he'd have if it seemed his girlfriend might leave him, something he had to stop "at any cost."

"He's doing Mavis," said Austin again.

Leo looked around wildly and suddenly stood up and left the room. The instructor quickly followed, telling us he would be right back.

We all sat there digesting Leo's interesting bit of information. Leo had not denied it. When the instructor came back he asked us all if we had a hot thought to discuss. He said nothing about Leo, and no one asked.

Into the growing silence came Bradley's voice. "It's like landing a plane in the fog with no instruments."

We all turned to look at him. He was staring at a point above and to the left of the instructor but when I looked, there was nothing but a blank cinderblock wall.

After a long moment of silence Bradley continued, "The plane is my mind trying to find solid ground, but the fog dulls all my senses. It disconnects everything and my brain is mush." He stopped talking.

We waited. Finally the instructor said, "And how does that make you feel?" The instructor stood by his easel, marker poised and ready.

"Desolate."

"Any other emotions?"

"When you're desolate what else is there? It's all empty," said Bradley.

The instructor sought refuge in his next question. "What automatic thoughts go through your head?"

"I will never get better because nothing works."

"And the evidence for that?"

"I've been medicated for two years and nothing works."

"And the evidence against that?"

Bradley stared at the instructor, who gently prodded Bradley with "Have you tried every possible medication?"

Bradley hesitated and then said, "No."

"So what is your balanced response to your statement that you will never get better because nothing works?"

Bradley leaned forward on his elbows, a glint of interest, or maybe excitement, in his eyes.

"If at first you don't succeed ... try something new," he said, sounding as if he had just made up his mind about something. He fell silent.

The instructor looked around and made eye contact with Kit. "Have you got a situation for us?" he asked.

She squirmed on her seat and then said in a rush, "I can't stop thinking that someone close to me is going to die."

"What happens when you think that? What do you feel?"

"Scared. I'm fixated on it. Obsessed with it. I have to do all these rituals, or it will happen."

"But you know it's an obsession."

"Yes, but I can't help myself. If I step on any lines, someone I love will die."

"Is that your hot thought?"

"Yes. Someone I love will die." She was wringing her hands in her lap.

"All right. What is the evidence that your hot thought could be right?"

"I saw someone. She looked dead. She was my friend." Her voice cracked on the word "friend."

"But she wasn't dead, was she?" said the instructor. It was a statement and not a question.

"I don't know. She went away."

"Okay," said the instructor. "You say she looked dead. Could she have been asleep and you just imagined she was dead, or you dreamed it?"

Kit's frown relaxed and she looked up and said, "Yes, that could be it." But she didn't look very certain.

"Have you tried calling her?"

"It just goes to voicemail."

"Have you contacted her family?"

"She doesn't have any."

"Friends, then?"

Kit shook her head.

"Okay, have you stepped on any lines since you had this thought about your friend?"

Kit looked worried and said, "Yes."

"And did anybody you love die?"

Dangerous question, I thought.

"No. At least, I don't think so," she said, but again she seemed unsure.

It was definitely not the response the instructor was looking for, but he was saved from having to do damage control by Austin, who was tapping his watch vigorously to indicate the session was over.

Can Kit have been talking about Mavis? I wondered as I got up to leave.

Bradley had scooted out of the conference room and I had to run to catch up with him. "Have to get a coffee," he said as if that would dismiss me. But when he realized I wasn't going to let him get a coffee all by himself, he said, "Coffee is a secret drug used by a higher order to control humans. Do you still want some?"

I nodded and we headed toward the common room, but he surprised me and went through the doors to the elevator, instead of getting the coffee from the cafeteria. I hadn't realized he was able to leave unescorted. He seemed so sick sometimes, but then I guess we all did. The elevator was pretty full and we were crammed into it as it stopped at every floor, and when at last it spewed us out, I was feeling quite claustrophobic. I followed him to the little coffee shop on the ground floor of the hospital. We each bought our own coffee and then went to sit at the coffee bar.

He looked at me as though I was supremely stupid, his long black hair cascading over his face. "Have you tasted the coffee upstairs?"

I laughed. "So it's only some coffee that controls our minds?"

He laughed, but his pale grey eyes didn't. "No, it's *all* coffee, but if I'm going to be controlled I might as well drink the good stuff."

"Why not give up coffee altogether?" I asked.

"You don't understand. It's everybody. It controls everybody. And it's addictive. So many people drink coffee that we have even named a break after it. Can't say that about milk or lemonade. It's synonymous with break time. And that's why it's so dangerous, because it's all pervasive, all persuasive. Only kids are immune and the odd person who doesn't like coffee. Coffee needs an antidote and I'm working on that."

"What sort of antidote?"

"One that banishes delusions like mine."

"Is that what you gave to Mavis?"

"What I gave to Mavis?" He was suddenly very still, like an animal sensing danger.

"The morning of her ECT. The day before she died," I said.

He looked furtive, but said nothing.

"I saw you give her something."

"It's the coffee making you say that. I can tell. You're lying."

"Or *you're* lying."

We were at an impasse, so I changed the subject. "What possesses a Scientologist to write about God's Disgrace?"

He looked down into his coffee mug, cradled in his hands, as if something there could guide him. He was a very long time in answering, but since I couldn't think of anything else to say to him, I waited patiently and watched as a little girl carefully carried her hot chocolate to a table with four other little girls and one harried-looking guy overseeing them all.

Finally I prodded him. "Which are you — a believer or an atheist?" I said. "Or maybe you are an agnostic?"

There must have been something really fascinating going on in his coffee mug because he didn't acknowledge that I had said anything. So I answered the question for him.

"Scientology would never let an agnostic into their midst. And why would you want to be there, anyway, if you were agnostic?"

He blinked at me.

"Maybe you were never a Scientologist. Maybe you were trying to get into Mavis's good books for some reason, and just pretended you were a Scientologist."

He blinked again.

"Were you in love with her? Did she refuse you? Is that why you killed her?"

There was no charitable way to say it. Bradley snickered. Okay. So, not in love with her. I tried to get some answers out of him, but he had clammed up. When he rose to leave I let him go, wishing I could have known what to say that would have unlocked him.

chapter nineteen

I had wanted to talk to Jacques after the CBT class, but he'd seemed in such a hurry to get out of there and then I'd pursued Bradley, so that there was no opportunity to talk. But Jacques had aroused my curiosity more than ever, and when I went back upstairs after my meeting with Bradley, I saw him heading for the elevators, so I decided to follow him and find out what he was up to. If I was falling for this guy I needed to know who he really was.

I ran and got my coat and boots. Of course, he could simply be going out to satisfy a smoking urge, in which case I could just walk to the Tim Hortons, pretend to get a coffee, and come back, so he wouldn't suspect I was following him. Again the elevator was so slow and so crowded. When it finally arrived at the first floor I ran out into winter and the street filled with snow and looked in both directions. Jacques was difficult to miss. He was a head taller than anyone else and his blond hair was not trapped by a hat, so it was blowing around like a lion's mane in a hurricane. He was heading east, and I followed at a discreet distance.

We passed the architecture building and the University of Toronto Bookstore and crossed St. George Street. He turned north on King's College Road and headed into the heart of the university. We passed the round dome of Convocation Hall and skirted the huge circular playing field that in summer was littered with people lazing on the grass or playing Frisbee or soccer.

Jacques didn't linger and I had to run to keep up with him. He didn't even look at the beautiful massive building of University College. In summer its age-old stones were almost hidden by a riotous amount of ivy, but now they were barren and cold, their roughened surfaces a mass of tiny shadows. Before us was the impressive stone Soldiers' Tower, whose bells ring out in a grand carillon in the summer months. He turned east just after the quaint little church-like building that houses the Student's Union, and then toward Hart House, its stone edifice warmed by the brilliant sunshine. He passed the main entrance of Hart House and then opened the door to the Arbor Room restaurant and went inside.

I waited a few minutes and followed him into the foyer. It took my eyes some seconds to adjust, but I caught sight of him through the foyer windows as he stood in line. I waited until he had bought some juice and a sandwich and brought it back to a table. Luck was with me. He took a seat with his back to me and I sidled in and took a seat as far away as I could get, but still keep him in sight. I picked up someone's discarded newspaper and pretended to read. I hoped I wouldn't get kicked out because I hadn't bought anything.

By the time he'd finished his lunch I was getting restive. I was afraid that if I got up to buy something to eat he would see me, or he would leave. Either scenario left me sitting there with a rumbling stomach.

I almost missed it. A tall, heavy-set balding man walked toward Jacques's table and stopped. He pulled out an envelope and handed it to Jacques. They talked for about thirty seconds and then the man left. I'd had enough. I pushed back my chair and headed toward Jacques.

He looked up in surprise as I pulled out the chair opposite him and sat down without an invitation.

"Cordi, how nice," he said and casually picked up the envelope and tucked it into an inside pocket.

"Who are you?" I asked.

He turned his head quizzically to one side. "Jacques," he said.

"I think you know what I mean," I said.

"No." He held the word for a long time and then said, "I'm not sure I'm following you, Cordi."

"You're hiding something. You're not a smoker because you're in too good physical shape. You weren't even winded on the stairs, and you knew about the subway and I hadn't told you. And when I asked you what poison you drank, you hesitated, as if you didn't know."

I stared at him, and he stared back.

"And Martha says you're acting," I added lamely.

Jacques splayed his huge hands on top of the table, shook his head, laughed, and homed in on the one piece of information that I didn't want him to.

"Martha? Why would she confide in you? You don't even know her."

I'd never been good at keeping a poker face.

"You do know her."

"Why would you jump to that conclusion?"

"Because you're hiding something," he said.

I was really angry with myself, and Martha was going to kill me. I had almost blown her cover trying to blow his.

We sat there facing each other, the tension rising with each passing second, until I could stand it no more.

"Are you trying to kill me?" You couldn't get blunter than that.

"Why would I want to do that?" he asked, looking baffled.

"Because you killed Mavis and think my snooping around will reveal you as a killer." I was watching him closely, looking for any telltale sign that he wasn't who he said he was, which come to think of it, was only "Jacques." Was that even his real name?

"But why would I kill Mavis?" he said, raising his hands in a gesture of utter mystification.

I hadn't thought this through very well. I had no real idea why he would want to kill Mavis, and Martha's suggestions seemed a little flimsy with Jacques sitting right across from me.

"Then maybe you're a private investigator or under-cover cop," I said. I had no idea where that came from. Somewhere out of my subconscious mind, I guess, although now that I thought about it, the guy who'd handed Jacques the envelope had had *cop* written all over him. He could have been Jacques's boss, giving him orders. Jacques raised his hands to his face, ostensibly to rub it, but it also served to hide his face so that I couldn't read anything there.

"Why would you think that?" he finally said, lowering his hands and looking me in the eye.

"Because you're so interested in helping me find Mavis's killer," I said.

"And you can't think of any other reason I might be interested?" He smiled. I was thankful at that moment that I am not prone to blushing, or I'd have looked like a boiled lobster.

"Cordi, you have a wild imagination." He paused. "Has it given you any ideas as to why Mavis was killed? At least, ideas that have nothing to do with me as the killer?"

I looked at him and twisted my mouth in a grimace. Was I going to let him change the subject? Was he really a danger to me? He certainly didn't seem like it.

When I didn't say anything, he continued. "I've been thinking about what you overhead Ella saying the other day. And by the way, you're not the only one to eavesdrop on the nurses," he said. "How else would I have known about the subway?"

I'd forgotten about that. The police could have told Ella everything.

"You said that she said there were others." Jacques went on, pulling me back from my thoughts.

"Yeah. Creepy."

"Creepy, but it may speak to motive. If there've been other suspicious deaths on the floor, maybe there's a serial killer on the loose, and you've been targeted."

"To keep me from finding out about the 'other' deaths and linking them to Mavis? Or to stop me from finding the truth about Mavis?"

Jacques nodded. "Both."

"So it could be a patient as a serial killer?"

"Could be, but it could also be a nurse or a doctor or a member of the cleaning staff."

"That puts us all in danger," I said. I drummed my fingers on the tabletop. "But that would make no sense."

"What would make no sense?"

"Why Ella, or whoever, isn't targeting me anymore."

"And why don't you think Ella is trying to kill you anymore, assuming it is Ella and not me?" asked Jacques with a smile.

"Because there haven't been any attempts on my life in a while," I said, meeting his gaze.

"But why would someone just stop like that?" he asked.

"Maybe the killer is a hired assassin," I said, watching to see how he reacted to that. But he didn't flinch.

"Maybe the assassin's employer had a change of heart," I said. "Or maybe the assassin just got too interested in his target."

Jacques didn't laugh. In fact, he didn't react at all until he said, "You'd be dead by now if it was a professional killer. They don't fail, at least not twice. Still doesn't explain why the attacks have stopped."

I shivered and then I told him about Austin and his rendezvous with a drug dealer.

"What if Mavis knew? He could have killed her to prevent anyone from knowing he was buying drugs."

"Or she could have been blackmailing him and he killed her to stop that," said Jacques.

"I thought about that," I countered, "but apparently Mavis was wealthy so why would she blackmail anyone?"

"Because she'd given all her money to Scientology?

"That's what Martha and I thought, but maybe we're just barking up the wrong tree."

"What's the right tree?" asked Jacques.

I shook my head and we lapsed into silence as we walked back together, Jacques and I, to the hospital. He was the perfect gentleman, keeping between the traffic and me and holding my arm to guide me safely across every intersection.

"So what was in the envelope?" I asked suddenly, hoping to catch him off guard.

"Tickets to the Habs game," he said without a pause. I wasn't sure I believed him, and why was he a Habs fan when he lived in Toronto?

"Habs game?" I asked.

"As in Montreal Canadiens."

"I knew that, but why are *you* a Habs fan?"

"Why is my name Jacques?"

He could be so infuriating, so I changed the subject. "What do you think of Leo and Mavis being a couple?" I asked, recalling the CBT meeting.

"Didn't see that coming," he said.

"Gives him some doozy motives, especially if they were living together long enough for him to be entitled to some or all of her stuff. For starters Mavis was wealthy. He could have been after her money."

"But why now?" said Jacques.

"She was threatening to leave him. Or maybe he needed to get rid of her before she gave all her money to Scientology." I was on a roll. "Or maybe it was because she actually did rebuff him. He felt like a failure and he was angry that, paraphrasing his words, someone like Mavis should be thankful to get anyone at all."

Jacques took my arm again as we crossed St. George Street. A car turning right cut us off and Jacques slammed his fist down on the hood, earning the finger from the driver.

With his hand on my arm, I'd lost my train of thought by the time we reached the safety of the curb.

"But Leo's so scared of everything," said Jacques, taking up the conversation as if there'd been no interruption. "He hears something even the least bit negative, blows it up out of all proportion, and winds up in a panic attack. I just can't see him murdering Mavis."

"Unless the alternative was worse."

"What do you mean?"

"Unless it's worse to be made to feel like a failure all the time. With Mavis out of the way he could get on with his life."

"I don't buy it," said Jacques. "The money aspect, yeah. That works for me. And maybe if Mavis knew something that Leo had to keep secret at all costs, such as maybe the 'other' murders, I could see him murdering her. He might have believed that she'd ruin his life."

"My point exactly. She was ruining his life, by his account. He worked himself into a panic almost every time he saw her."

We walked in silence for a while and I was aware that people were making space for us, as they never did when I walked alone and got crowded. Jacques's size forced respect, even from total strangers.

"I thought Bradley's comment was intriguing," I said.

"About being desolate. Yeah, that was pretty sad."

"No, I mean what he said about trying again."

"I think he was just talking about maybe trying a medication again."

"Yes, that's what I thought. But he said it as if he'd made up his mind about something. Something specific."

"Hmm," said Jacques. "Maybe he's got some weird

serial-killer mentality where killing makes him feel good temporarily. He killed Mavis to feel good and is now thinking of striking again."

"That's macabre."

We were almost at the hospital when Jacques turned and asked me about Martha and how I knew her. "Does mental illness run in your circle of friends?" he asked, but I detected a note of disbelief in his voice.

"She's going to kill me," I said. "No one is supposed to know she's an old friend."

"Why not?"

I realized my mistake. He didn't know anything more than that we were friends. Nothing hugely suspicious about that. He didn't know she was faking, and now he might wonder.

"She's a very private person," I said lamely.

"Her secret's safe with me," he said, and I realized I had no way of knowing if it was or why it really mattered. After all, if Martha really needed help, who would care if we were old friends? But if I was talking to the murderer it was a whole different story. I could be endangering Martha.

I changed the subject and told him about the strange thing Kit had said in an unguarded moment. "'I saw her lying there.' What did she mean by that? That she saw her lying there, alive or dead, or awake or asleep?"

"No idea," said Jacques.

"But if she saw Mavis dead, why wouldn't she say so?"

"What makes you think she saw her dead?"

"Just the way she said it. It was creepy, and the way she talked in CBT about seeing a dead friend? What was that all about? Could it have been Mavis?"

"Maybe she didn't see her dead, but she saw something else," said Jacques.

And it suddenly dawned on me. "Kit is the only one who always speaks of Mavis in the past tense."

"So do I," said Jacques. "So do you."

I glanced up at him quickly, but his face was unreadable. "Why do you speak of her in the past tense?"

"Because I believe you?"

chapter twenty

Next morning after breakfast I went back to my room to lie down. I intended to have a nap, but I couldn't, because Martha was sitting on my bed, looking out the window.

"Hi, stranger," she said in what sounded like an accusatory voice.

So I told her about following Jacques and asking him if he was trying to murder me.

"What did he say to that?" she asked.

"He didn't really. So I asked him point-blank if he was an undercover cop."

"A cop? Are you kidding me?"

"Why not? It makes perfect sense. And you were the one who said he was acting."

"So he comes undercover looking to flush out Mavis's murderer?" she asked. "But that doesn't make sense. Kit told me he was here before Mavis died."

So I told her about "the others."

"He could have been looking into these other murders when Mavis died," I said. "After all, he was the one to first suggest that Mavis's death was covered up."

"Or maybe there weren't any other murders and he was just hired to kill Mavis," said Martha.

Put like that it sounded pretty awful. Jacques seemed like such a great guy.

"Maybe he was hired for some other reason that relates to Mavis," I said, clutching at straws.

"So what did he say about being a cop?"

"He sort of just changed the subject."

"Does that sound like an innocent man?"

I didn't answer and she said, "If he's an undercover cop he hasn't exactly done very much, has he? I mean, you seem to be doing all the work."

"He's *undercover*, Martha. As in incognito. Sort of like you."

"Why are you defending him?"

I hesitated. "He's a good man," I finally said, the hope in my voice noticeable even to me.

Martha eyeballed me and said, "Lord love a duck, Cordi. Have you fallen for him?"

I didn't say anything, couldn't say anything, and she stared at me for a long time before changing the subject.

"I've been busy, too," she said.

I rolled my eyes, thankful she hadn't given me the second degree, and wondered what kind of trouble Martha had got herself into.

"I hid in the men's washroom," she said.

"You what?" I said, totally taken off guard. "What's wrong with the women's washroom?"

"It doesn't have men in it, obviously."

"Obviously."

"Besides, the cleaners were in the women's and I didn't want to disturb them, and the men's was empty.

"Anyway, I was in the stall and Bradley came in, followed by Austin. They were each standing at a urinal. I could see through the crack in the door."

"Jesus, Martha!"

"Cripes, Cordi, I wasn't interested in what they were doing! I was interested in what they were saying."

"The suspense is killing me."

"Bradley said, 'I've got it for you,' and then Austin said, 'Will it work?' and Bradley answered, 'It'll stop it from happening.'" Martha stopped talking and smiled at me.

"Is that all?" I asked, not sure what to make of the information.

"Isn't it enough?"

"Well, I'm not sure what it means. Are you certain it was Bradley who said, 'I've got it,' and not Austin?"

She looked at me blankly. I was pretty sure I'd told her about Austin and the drugs, but I told her again.

"No, it was Bradley," she said after I'd finished.

"So what did Bradley have that Austin wanted and that would stop something from happening?"

"An aspirin?" suggested Martha.

I looked at her and grimaced and she smiled back at me.

"What can I say? It was the first thing that came to my mind."

I debated whether to tell her that Jacques knew she was my old friend. In the end I kept it to myself. I didn't need to have my head chewed off.

—

I was staring out the window when Ella breezed into my room.

"Dr. Osborn wants to see you in twenty minutes," she said.

This time Ella didn't wait for me and I waited ten minutes before I headed toward the cafeteria and the door to the doctors' offices. I was nine minutes early but I figured I could hang out in the hall and think, instead of having to talk to Kit, who had just returned from CBT. Someone had propped the door to the cafeteria open with a wooden wedge and I went on through and down the hall to Osborn's office. His door was slightly ajar and I couldn't resist taking a peek, wondering what patient was in there with him.

But it wasn't a patient.

It was Ella. And she was crying.

I jumped back, worried that I had been seen, and crept back down the hall to the cafeteria where I waited another five minutes before approaching Osborn's door again. He was sitting at his desk, writing in a folder and scanning the computer, seemingly at the same time. He smiled up at me and asked me to take a seat. There was classical music playing in the background and as usual the lighting was warm and cozy — he'd turned off the overheads and left the floor lamps lit. After a moment he got up and came and sat in the chair across from me, holding a folder in one hand and a pen in the other. He looked sombre and determined, which could not be good.

He said, "Cordi, I understand that you continue to upset a number of the patients with your version of what happened to Mavis."

"No one will believe me," I said.

"No. People don't understand. There's a difference. Whether they believe you or not is irrelevant if they don't understand." I blinked at him.

"The way I see it," he said, "you have two problems. The first is depression. There is a lot of stigma out there that depression can be fixed if you just suck it up and pull up your socks. As you know everybody has experienced depression in its mild form — sadness — and so everyone feels they are experts, when, in fact, they have no idea what depression is in the clinical sense."

He reached forward and slid the folder onto the coffee table in front of him. "Clinical depression really needs a new term to distinguish it from the depression most people have felt at one time or other, saying they're having a down day, a bummer day, or feel blue or in the dumps or are in a funk." He pressed his fingertips together and touched them to his mouth.

"Desolation would be a better term," he said. "Most people would never describe their depression as desolation, except those who are truly desolate. You've been there. You know what I'm talking about."

I nodded.

"To be desolate is to be clinically depressed," he said.

"So you're saying the word 'depression' is like the word 'awesome'? It's been watered down?"

"Exactly. A person can be a little bit depressed or blue, or a lot depressed and suicidal. It's a huge range. 'Desolate' is an absolute. You are in a cold dark place if you are desolate, unable to be cheered up by others."

I was wondering where he was going with this when he suddenly said, "You aren't depressed anymore, but your delusions are taking over your life."

"I am not delusional!" I said angrily. "I saw Mavis and she was dead and someone is trying to kill me because of that information. I am just protecting myself."

"Delusions are not your fault," he said, maddeningly calm. "But if you really believe, say, that someone is after you, everything you do to stop that from happening might be logical, but the premise is false. No one is after you. And people don't understand."

Curious choice of words, I thought. Certainly not very subtle. And I'd gone over the whole premise in my mind many times before, but always as it related to others. Was Osborn suggesting this to me to cover his own back? Had *he* killed Mavis?

"I'm concerned about you," he said. "I think you might have some kind of delusional disorder."

I felt another surge of anger rip through me. How dared this man tell me my world was not real. But then, it was just what he might say if he'd murdered Mavis and was trying to cover it up.

"I don't believe aliens control my brain!" I snapped. "Or that my watch speaks to me!"

He waved a hand dismissively. "That's not what I mean. Your delusions are not bizarre the way they are in schizophrenia. They could actually happen in the real world. Mavis could have died."

"She *did* die, though, and you and the cops and the hospital are covering it up for some reason."

I knew he was lying to me. I knew what I had seen, and it was as real as the air I was breathing.

"Have there been other episodes in your past where people haven't believed you?"

I was so astounded that I couldn't answer. I thought

back to my trip to the Arctic on the *Susannah Moodie* when Martha, Duncan, and I had solved a murder. Martha and Duncan hadn't believed me when I told them someone was out to get me. But I had been right. And it was depression that gripped me from time to time, not something more sinister. Not that depression wasn't awful all by itself.

"If not," Osborn went on, "then it could just be manifesting itself for the first time. We need to talk about your delusions, Cordi."

He might have needed to talk about them, but I could see right through him. He really just wanted to know how much I knew about Mavis's death and the cover-up. And I wasn't talking. Someone must have been watching over me, though, because we were interrupted by a knock on the door and I didn't have to answer him. Dr. Osborn went to the door, opened it, and then looked swiftly at me, said he'd be back in a minute and left, leaving the door ajar.

I looked at the file folder on the table. I wanted to pick it up, but I was worried Osborn would come back. I got up and went over to a bookshelf behind the sofa. There was a picture of a younger-looking Osborn posing with what I presumed were his wife and son and daughter.

I went back to the coffee table, took a chance, and picked up the folder. The patient's name was Minnie Addison. She was an Alzheimer's patient, but not Osborn's. She had died in hospital several years ago under the care of a Dr. David Ellison, whose name rang a bell. *Ah, yes.* Osborn's co-author on research papers regarding cognitive behavioural therapy, Alzheimer's, and memory loss. I dropped the folder back onto the table, worried that Osborn would catch me snooping again, and wondered why he was interested in someone with memory loss who had died several years ago.

Osborn returned a few minutes later and sat opposite me.

"Cordi, as I said, I'm concerned that your medication —" He was interrupted yet again, this time by the phone, and apologized profusely, but when he went to check who it was, he said he had to take the call. Of course, I couldn't help but overhear. He was talking to someone he knew well, because the warmth and concern in his voice was apparent.

"Look, we've been through this a thousand times before. There's nothing I can do. It's been stopped. It's out of my hands." He paused and then said, "You know I've done everything possible and I'll keep doing everything possible. You know that, don't you?"

I glanced at Osborn's face. He was frowning as he hung up and said nothing for a while, and then he started, looked at me, and said, "Where were we? Oh, yes, we may need to change your medication in light of your new symptoms."

"I think my medication's working," I said. "I'm not in a really dark space anymore."

"No, but as I said, it's not just the depression we have to worry about. I want to add a new medication. See if it helps. Have you thought some more about another ECT if things should worsen?"

One look at my face and he sighed.

"An ECT could help you, Cordi. It did once already, so don't reject it out of hand." He was being very persistent.

"But it could destroy my memory again." I paused and then asked, "Is there any drug out there that could help memory loss from ECT?"

He hesitated and pursed his lips. "Nothing on the market that really works," he said, which wasn't really an answer, and then rather abruptly, "All right, then. We'll start you on a low dose of a new medication and hopefully that will help."

And that was the end of the interview.

I was curious about Osborn and went to the closet of a computer room to see what I could find out about him. I googled his name and came up with some really prolific real-estate agent, so I tunnelled down until I found entries for a Dr. Richard Osborn, psychiatrist. He'd written two papers on Alzheimer's and a couple on CBT, as well as one on ECT, which confirmed what I'd seen on his desk. I couldn't get abstracts for any of the papers, so I wrote down their titles with the intention of looking them up at Robarts Library at the University of Toronto. I was just finishing when the door opened and I looked up to see Austin standing there.

"Sorry," he said, and started backing away.

"It's okay. I'm just finishing."

He stood in the doorway and watched as I gathered together my stuff.

"You know," he said, "I didn't really kill her."

I looked up. "I know."

"How do you know?"

"No police came to arrest you. That, and because you didn't mention the scarf."

"The scarf," he said, as if it was an afterthought and not a surprise. I waited for him to explain, which he did. "Everybody knew about the scarf. Everybody but the doctors and nurses. Lucy kept it as a talisman and as a finger to the staff that she could hide a dangerous object from them. Anyway, I couldn't sleep and I was passing Mavis's room when I heard a sound. The door was open and I looked in."

Pretty much what he had said before and I marvelled again at how easy it was to walk the halls without a nurse accosting him. So much for our safety, but then, I had done it myself. The fact that our door was open was not unusual. The room was so stuffy we often left the door open once the nurses had checked on us in the night. Just creepy that someone was watching us as we slept.

I waited.

"So I went inside and stood over Mavis. She was lying on her back and she was wide awake, her mouth shaping up for a scream, so I pressed the pillow to her face and held it there." He hadn't mentioned the business about her mouth being open before and I wondered where he was going with it. Was Mavis already dead when he tried to smother her?

"But you just said you didn't kill her," I said.

"It was just a delusion. That's what Dr. Osborn says."

"So you never saw the scarf?"

"That's not what I said. I went back to my room, but I couldn't get it out of my head that maybe I hadn't killed her. I needed to check. I mean, she hadn't resisted, so maybe I'd dreamt it all. And the voices were so insistent that I check. When I went back I did the same thing. I looked in through the crack of the door. At first I couldn't see, but then my eyes adjusted and I saw Kit — you can't miss her wild red hair — holding a scarf in her hands as she knelt by Mavis's bed. She took the scarf and wrapped it gently and lovingly around Mavis's neck and then gave her a hug."

"Why would she do that?" I asked.

"Beats me," said Austin.

"Was she blackmailing you?" I asked on impulse.

Austin jerked his head away from me. "I beg your pardon?"

"Was Mavis blackmailing you?"

"Why would she do that?"

"Because she knew about your drug habit."

Austin backed out through the doorway to the hall. "You're crazy, you know that?"

"I saw you in Kensington Market," I said.

He turned to walk down the hall, but not before I saw the anger on his face. Why the hell would he be angry? The emotion I expected was fear, not anger, unless he was angry at me for being so nosy. Even so, fear should have been his first emotion. It was interesting that it was not. Maybe he was getting drugs from Bradley and what I saw in Kensington Market was something else. But how was I supposed to ask him that?

"You don't know anything," he said.

He was absolutely right.

chapter twenty-one

I was really restive and decided to go to Robarts Library to look up Osborn's papers. I signed myself out and took the seven flights of stairs down to the ground floor, figuring anybody who was following me would have to follow me down the stairs. Once on the ground level I waited just outside the stairwell door to see if anyone emerged, but no one did, so I headed outside. Nothing had happened to me for some days and I was thinking that whoever it was had changed their mind for some reason and struck me off their kill list. It had snowed in the night and the sidewalk up Huron Street had not yet been cleared by the little snowploughs. I made the little jog at Russell Street and headed on up past the Ramsay Wright Zoological Laboratories.

I came out at Harbord Street and there, in all its strangeness, was the monolith that was Robarts. It was like some giant piece of concrete plunked down beside single-family dwellings and a little corner store that used to sell fantastic spiced chicken legs. The wide stone diagonal stairway up to the main entrance was daunting, even to an athlete. As I walked up the stairs I had the unnerving feeling of wanting to walk on the diagonal to conform with the stairs. The building soared fourteen stories, looking periscopic and standing on an unusual footprint that weaved and turned like a sidewinder. It was reminiscent of a Lego set, with mere slits of windows on the higher levels, and on the lower levels chunky, blocky windows snapped onto the face seemingly at random.

I reached the top of the twenty-eight stairs and went inside. As weird as the outside was, the inside was utilitarian except for the three-foot-long candle-shaped lights hanging from the ceiling of the tiled lobby. It had been a long time since I'd used the library, but I knew the drill and took the elevator up to the stacks to retrieve the research papers. It took awhile but finally I had the four journals I was after in hand and spent the next fifteen minutes photocopying Osborn's articles.

After that I got a coffee in the cafeteria and sat there gazing into space for a while, thinking about Mavis. I began to pull out the papers I'd photocopied from my bag where I'd stashed them.

And suddenly something jumped into my space and bit me.

I'd glanced out through the cafeteria's interior windows at a set of escalators and seen two women in a passionate kiss. I looked away, not wanting them to catch me staring. When I glanced back, they had parted from each other and were talking animatedly. I could see their faces clearly, and I suppose I shouldn't have been so startled because there had been lots of clues: Kit and Lucy.

I recalled that day in the bathroom when Kit had said, "Why are you doing this?" I'd thought it was about the toilet paper, but it must have been a lovers' quarrel.

Now Kit said something that made Lucy turn to look at me. I smiled thinly. I watched as they conferred with one another and then headed toward the cafeteria, Kit avoiding the golden lines on the tiled floor. When they reached me Kit sat down, but Lucy stayed standing.

"So you know," said Lucy.

I shrugged as I looked up at her.

"It won't go well for us if they find out at the hospital," she said, her face impassive. Kit was flicking some non-existent lint off her coat.

"They can't know," said Kit. "They won't let us be together. No romances allowed on the floor."

"They'll transfer one of us off the floor," said Lucy.

"Is that so bad?" I asked.

"Yeah, it is. We've done the rounds and this is the best place in town."

"What do you mean, you've 'done the rounds'?"

"When you're in and out of hospital a lot you get sent to different places, but you see a lot of the same people, and this place is the best."

"You can't tell," pleaded Kit.

"Is that what Mavis did? Threatened to tell? So you killed her?"

"Oh, Jesus," said Lucy. "Are we back to Mavis again?" She looked at me and then at Kit. "Mavis got sick," said Lucy. "Period."

"Is that what you think, Kit?" I asked.

She nodded.

"Then why did you put the scarf around her neck?"

Kit froze, then asked, her face a picture of fear and surprise, "How did you know that?" She looked at Lucy, who was uncharacteristically quiet.

"Was she dead?" I asked.

Kit looked at me, obviously struggling to find a way to answer. Finally she said, "I thought maybe she was. So I had to tidy her up. Make her look peaceful and nice."

"Did you tell anyone?" I asked.

Kit looked at Lucy, who looked startled. "No," said Kit in a tiny voice. "How did you know?"

Suddenly Lucy made a chopping motion with her hand. "Forget the fucking scarf," she said harshly. "What's it to anyone, anyway?" She glared at me. "Will you keep our secret?"

"What will you do if I don't?" I asked.

"Oh, shit. You are unbelievable. Would it help if I say I'll cut you into little bits and dump you down the sewer?"

"Lucy, that's no way to get her to keep our secret," said Kit in a plaintive voice.

"Would you please not tell?" said Lucy in a sugary voice.

I looked at Kit. "As long as it doesn't hurt anybody."

"Little Miss Righteous," said Lucy as Kit got up and pulled her away. They were an odd pair, with Kit not even reaching Lucy's shoulder in height.

I watched them walk out of the lobby together, slowing down so Kit could avoid the lines, and thought about happiness and how elusive it was.

No one followed me back to the hospital. I was too late for lunch, so I stopped at the first-floor cafeteria, where I bought a sandwich and some juice and sat by the window and watched the people walk by. My mind was a jumble of facts, thoughts, theories, and suppositions. There were so many possibilities that I felt scattered and unsure of myself. I finished my lunch and went up to the seventh floor, signed myself in, and went to bed, hoping a nap might help. But I couldn't doze off.

My mind was racing and I couldn't slow it down. I couldn't even concentrate enough to read Osborn's articles. I needed to do something. Anything. And that was when I remembered that I needed more clothes and decided to go home for a quick visit.

I signed myself out and took the subway, spending a lot of anxious moments looking over my shoulder, but I made it home in one piece and gathered some clothes, more shampoo, and another towel. I had brought laundry home with me, laundry I hadn't wanted to wash in the machines on the floor because I was afraid they would chew up my clothes. It had happened to me before with a strange machine, so I was taking no chances.

I threw the laundry in the machine in the room next to the bathroom and went to check the fridge. It was full of spoiled food, so I began checking the cupboards. Then the doorbell rang. I went to red alert. Should I answer it? What if my killer was there? Who else could it be? I crept up to the front door and listened, hoping for a clue. Instead the doorbell rang again and a man's voice said, "Cordi, are you there?" I put the chain on the door and opened it a crack. And there stood Jacques, his finger poised over the bell.

He smiled at me and said, "I followed you home."

His voice was velvet and roller-coaster sexy, but I was caught in an awful moment of uncertainty. It was more than obvious why he was at my door by the come-hither look in his eye, but did he have an ulterior motive? Was he leading me on only to murder me in a post-coital slumber? I opened the door and looked into his eyes and decided I didn't care about anything except the coital part as he cupped my face in both his hands and kissed me. And I kissed him back as I reached up and looped my arms around his neck. His hands on my waist, he pulled me closer and we stood entwined, until he suddenly put one arm under my knees and swooped me up into his arms.

"Where's your bedroom?" he whispered.

His hot breath seared my neck as he nibbled on my ear and carried me to the bedroom. He put me down gently by the bed and pushed me up against my dresser, the power of his body against mine made all the more powerful by his gentleness as he kissed me. His fingertips caressed my throat, brushing my breasts, and then he swung me around in one graceful movement and pushed me down onto the bed. His tongue danced around mine in a wild paroxysm of desire and anticipation as we undressed each other. His hands were as light and gentle as the wings of a butterfly. Curving over a breast, sliding down the hollow of my belly button, and over the Mound of Venus, while my fingers danced all over him. We melted into kisses, we melted into caresses, we melted into the moment, and nothing else. Suspended in time.

Suddenly he pulled back from me, his naked body a work of art in the sunbeam crossing my bed. His gaze searched every inch of my body, as if he was making love to me with his eyes. And then he was on top of me, the rhythm of our racing hearts beating against the rhythm of our bodies. Everything was distilled down to one shuddering moment of total vulnerability and surrender.

chapter twenty-two

Jacques refused to take the subway and insisted on taking a taxi back to the hospital. We sat snuggled in the back and talked about the little things that make a relationship big and strong. Neither of us mentioned Mavis. In the lobby he left to go and get a coffee, and I went up to my room to unpack my clean clothes, smiling all the while. Jacques had unloaded my laundry for me, giving me a running commentary of what he saw there and stating, in his sexy voice, that I really didn't need any of it.

I sat on my bed for a while hugging my memories, but I got restless after a time. I got up and went prowling down the hall and ended up in the art room. I hadn't been before because I hadn't known it existed. It was an organized chaos of a room with one huge long table in the centre, windows on two walls letting in the light, and cupboards and cabinets along three walls, paint-stained and obviously much used. Unlike every other bare wall on the floor, this room was full of the artwork of patients. I walked around looking at the images. There was a painting of a single woman in silhouette sitting at the top of some stairs, backlit and framed by the naked branches of a tree that crisscrossed behind her like cracked glass. And there was a poem surrounded by images of the devil with his forked tail and flickering tongue. I read the poem and wondered if it was Bradley's:

> Life's carousel was made by hell
> But Jesus has the bill of sale.

Idly I picked up some chalk and a piece of paper and went and sat on one of the stools snugged up under the table. The table itself was a work of art, covered in paint from the jars and minds of many a patient before me. I shuddered.

"Cold?" The voice startled me and I whirled around. Martha was standing in the doorway, the sun gleaming off her curly hair. I didn't answer and she came and sat beside me.

"You doing okay?" she asked. Why was everyone always asking me that? It was infuriating.

I nodded, hoping she wouldn't notice that I was feeling happier than I had felt in a long long time.

"You?' I said.

"Okay, I guess. It's hard being in here."

"Why's that?"

"Because you start to blend in," she said.

It was not what I'd wanted to hear, but I couldn't very well ignore it.

"What do you mean?" I asked.

"All this despair, all this sadness. It's getting to me. I don't feel I have to act anymore. It's unnerving."

"But you *are* acting, Martha. Don't let the place get to you."

"Thing is, my brother was bipolar and I remember his pain as being bottomless." So that was how she'd known so much about depression. It wasn't just me.

I reached over and hugged her and she hugged me back. "You're just acting," I said again, wishing I could say the same about myself.

"Awww. Isn't that nice to be such old friends?" We both turned in unison to see Jacques standing in the doorway, a toothpick hanging out of his mouth.

Martha drew away from me, her face one of complete surprise.

I watched as Jacques's face began to mirror Martha's and he said, "Oh, I'm sorry. I forgot." He smiled at me and I smiled back.

Martha looked at me and said, "You told him we were friends? Why would you do that?"

"It just slipped out," I said.

"Don't worry, I haven't told anyone else," said Jacques. "Not that it really matters."

He saw my quizzical glance and said, "Just because you two are old friends doesn't change anything, does it? Mental illness does not discriminate. Right?"

I wondered if he had been eavesdropping on us, but even more I remembered that I hadn't technically blown Martha's cover by telling him we were old friends. No one but me knew she was faking it to help me.

"Are you a cop?" Martha said suddenly.

Jacques pushed away from the doorjamb, walked into the room, and raised his hands in self-defence. "I've been called worse things in my life," he said, and then quickly, "What's new?"

I didn't answer right away. He didn't really look like a cop. Not with the longish hair. But he could be an undercover cop or a private investigator. After all, he'd had lock picks. Why hadn't I brought it up in bed? Surely he would have given me a straight answer. But I knew the answer to that. We had both been too busy.

"You mean, what's new about Mavis?" I finally asked.

"Is there something new?" He sat down across from us and I looked at Martha as his foot homed in on mine. I looked at him and he winked.

"There seems to be a lot of people who might have wanted her dead," I said, trying to keep my mind from wandering. I told him and Martha about Lucy and Kit, and Kit wrapping her scarf around Mavis's neck.

"So Mavis was already dead?" asked Jacques.

"Kit seemed to think so," I said.

"Do you believe her about just trying to tidy Mavis up?" asked Martha.

"Well," I said, "we know the scarf wasn't the murder weapon, so her story is plausible, if bizarre."

"So either Lucy or Kit could have smothered her to shut her up if she knew about them and was blackmailing them," said Martha.

"They were pretty upset about the thought of being separated, and Lucy reacted strangely when I asked her if Mavis was blackmailing her," I said. But looking back, I thought it could have been just a hiccup. Or not.

"Upset enough to kill?" asked Jacques.

I bit my lip and shrugged. "There's another possibility," I said.

They waited.

"What if there was a love triangle? What if Lucy and Kit were lovers but Mavis stole one of them away?"

"That would give either one another and more powerful motive to get rid of Mavis," said Jacques.

"Exactly," I said.

Martha looked dubious. "How does a love triangle happen in two weeks? Lucy told me she's been here the longest and that's just three weeks."

"She also told me that patients are often in and out of hospital, so they could all have known each other before," I said.

Jacques drummed his fingers on the table and then said, "Okay, let's recap the other scenarios. Austin may have been blackmailed by Mavis over drugs? Is that what you said, Cordi?"

I nodded.

"Where does Bradley fit in?" he asked next.

"So far, all I've come up with is his link to Scientology and therefore to Mavis," I said.

"Meaning?"

"I've been thinking about it a lot. Suppose Mavis had left Scientology so that she could be admitted to the hospital for help, and Bradley was sent to the hospital to bring her back. I've read that that's the sort of thing they do. When she refuses, he kills her."

"Pretty drastic," said Martha.

"Yeah, I guess," I said. "But religion has been used to justify some pretty drastic things."

Both Jacques and Martha nodded, and then Martha had another idea. "Or more likely, Bradley had left Scientology and Mavis was trying to get him to come back. He felt cornered, with no way out, so he smothered her in her sleep to get rid of her."

"I don't think the brass at Scientology would bother trying to get them back unless they were staff or someone high up, from what I've read about it," said Jacques. "Besides, Bradley said in CBT that he *is* a Scientologist." He took the toothpick out of his mouth with a flourish and tossed it in a nearby wastebasket.

"He could have been lying," I said. "I don't peg him as a Scientologist. His poetry shows him as agnostic, if not an atheist." I told them about Bradley's poems and the conversation I'd had with him.

"Why would he lie about something like that?" asked Jacques.

"I told him that maybe he was just trying to get into Mavis's good books."

"Why would he want to do that?" asked Martha.

"I don't know," I said, "but it must have been pretty important to him to put on such a front."

I was doodling on my sheet of paper and a horse with a bareback rider had blossomed under my pen.

Jacques reached over and took it from me. "Wow," he said, his voice full of wonder. "You can draw."

I laughed and took it back. "Suppose," I said, "it isn't anybody at the hospital at all?"

"Meaning?" asked Martha.

"Lucy told me that Mavis was really wealthy. That her parents died in a car crash from a blown tire. That Mavis was in the car, but she survived."

"And Mavis inherited everything?" asked Jacques.

"Yeah," I said. "But suppose it wasn't an accident. Suppose someone had tampered with the tire. Everybody was supposed to die and all the wealth would go to the killer."

Jacques thrummed the table with his fingers "Who is…?"

I shook my head. "I haven't got that far."

"Then let's deal with what we know," said Martha.

"Okay," said Jacques. "So that's Kit and Lucy, Bradley and Austin. And Leo could have killed Mavis for her money or in a moment of rage to assuage his battered ego, or a bit of both."

"It's possible that in the heat of the moment, he could have killed her," I said, an image of Lucy and Kit jumping into my head. "What if it really was a love triangle and Mavis really was having an affair with Kit or Lucy and Leo found out?"

"That could be more than just a battered ego," said Jacques. "There'd be a whole lot of soul-searching there, I think. He likely never would've thought that his competition came from a woman. No telling what that might have triggered in him."

"There's still the suicide option," said Martha. "Mavis could have OD'd on something."

"And they spirited her away so we wouldn't have to deal with her death?" I said.

"Something like that," said Martha.

"There's also the option that she actually just got sick the way they said, from a diabetic coma or something," said Jacques, looking at me pointedly, as if I should react. When I didn't he changed the subject. "What about Dr. Osborn?" he asked.

"What about him?" I asked.

"Maybe he had something to do with her death," Jacques suggested.

"What do you mean?" I was interested to get his take on it.

"He was her doctor. He controlled her medications. Easy enough to overdose her, I would think."

"But what possible motive would he have had?" asked Martha.

"And there would have been an inquest," I said.

Jacques looked at me and said, "There would've been an investigation no matter what happened to her. A young woman in apparent good health dies on a psych ward. Even if it was an untraceable drug that killed her, they still would have investigated. We're just not in the loop."

"But Osborn's still here," I said. "They would have arrested him by now." I looked back and forth between Martha and Jacques. "So she must have died from what looked like natural causes. And they were just good at covering up and hiding it all from us."

There was a flash of impatience on Jacques's face and Martha looked bemused.

"Even if it was an untraceable drug," I said, "the nurses know the medications that each person gets. They'd be suspicious."

"So Osborn had an accomplice?" asked Jacques. "Is that what you're saying?"

"Ella?" I suggested.

"She'd work as well as anyone, especially if she's the one who's been trying to kill you."

I thought back to Ella's little smile when Osborn took her by the arm, and I told them about it.

They both looked at me in surprise.

"So she kills Mavis to somehow save her man?" said Jacques. "A time-honoured tradition." Then he quickly added, "Not murder, but leaping to the defence of your man."

"You think they're lovers?" said Martha.

"It did pop into my head," I said. "But why has she stopped trying to kill me?"

"Has she?" asked Martha.

I glanced at Jacques. "No one has tried anything for ages, so either I am no longer a threat to Ella because something, or someone, has changed her mind about me, or whoever it is has, for some reason, moved on."

"Slow down," said Martha. "You're talking too fast. Why would the killer move on when whatever was bothering him was so troubling that he was willing to commit murder? Maybe something changed, as you say, or maybe he's just biding his time," said Martha.

Martha and I looked at Jacques at the same time. He looked taken aback.

"You still think I'm trying to kill you?" he asked in a wounded voice. He was our last suspect, after all, but I was confused and didn't want to be having this conversation. What kind of cruel luck gives you a lover on one hand and a killer on the other? It couldn't be Jacques.

"It did occur to us," said Martha.

"And where do you stand now?"

"Jury's still out?" said Martha.

Jacques looked at me, but I looked away. "Then why are you talking to me?"

"Trying to flush you out?" said Martha.

"Enough, guys," I said. "No offence, Jacques, but the only person I trust implicitly right at the moment is Martha." I didn't know Jacques well enough to think otherwise.

"As it should be," he said. "As it should be." But I could tell he was hurt.

Late in the afternoon Ella silently slid into my room, gave me an envelope, and left without a word. I opened the envelope to find a card and suddenly remembered that it was my birthday. I had gone through almost the entire day without remembering. Ryan had picked out a silly card with a cute cartoon dog jumping out of some tall grass to say Happy Birthday. He had scrawled an invitation to dinner tonight. *Pretty short notice*, I thought, a bit miffed, but then, maybe Ella had just forgotten to give it to me.

I was torn. I didn't feel much like talking to anybody, but it would be my family, and if I couldn't be myself with them, then with whom? In the end I accepted, and Ryan came and got me and drove me to his home. The streets were slushy and so the traffic was bad, and it took us longer than usual to get to his place. We didn't say a thing the whole way. But it was an easy silence, a brother-sister kind of silence that comes from years of knowing each other. And then I walked into his kitchen.

I know Ryan went to a lot of trouble. Wanted to cheer me up. But he had turned it into a surprise party with all my friends, which just made me want to cry. It was all I could do to put on a happy face and when I'd had enough I escaped to Ryan's study.

Unfortunately someone else had had the same idea He was a complete stranger to me. He was thin and short and the top of his head was bald, but he had grown out the circlet and combed the hair up and over the bald spot. It looked ridiculous, because it said so much about him that he should have wanted to keep private — like that he cared so much about his appearance. His eyes, when he turned them upon me, were dark and moist and heavy-lidded.

"You, too, eh?" he said in a high-pitched voice.

I grimaced and he laughed. "Isn't the birthday girl supposed to be the heart of the party?"

"Not when she doesn't have a heart." It came out sounding weird, even to me but I was frustrated at finding someone in my brother's study, and it was the first thing that came to mind for some reason. He looked at me more closely, as if trying to gauge whether or not I was joking.

He introduced himself as Brent Sebastien. He could apparently not help adding that he was a noted psychiatrist and a friend of one of my friends out in the kitchen. He'd come with her.

Just my luck to be stuck in the study with a "noted" psychiatrist. Until I realized maybe I could make something of it, if the stars aligned.

"Then you must know the noted Dr. Osborn," I said with an emphasis on "noted."

"Richard Osborn?"

I nodded.

"Yeah, I know of him. He was doing some bad-ass experiments on a miracle memory pill. Didn't work, I hear. Had to shut it down." He laughed in a moment of pure *schadenfreude*. I gagged on a sudden intake of breath.

"Too bad about his wife," he said after my coughing fit died down. "She was the best part of him. When his patient's husband slit her throat in the waiting room, he almost quit psychiatry."

"What stopped him?" I asked, trying not to gag again on the image he had given me.

"His son, I think. There was something funny there, just rumours, so I can't say, but I think his son kept him going."

"Little children can do that," I said, fishing.

"Oh, no, his son is in his late teens, maybe twenties by now. And Osborn remarried."

He stopped talking and so did I. We almost glared at each other until he gave in first.

"I'm not a gossip," he said, "and why are you so interested?"

"He's a business colleague of mine," I said, improvising. "He's been acting a bit odd lately and I was worried."

"I wouldn't be. He's a tough nut."

"But I thought you said he almost quit psychiatry."

"Yeah, he almost quit *psychiatry* because of his almost uncontrollable anger, but not life. There is a difference and he's a survivor." On that note Brent Sebastien saluted me and left, and I was all alone in a houseful of people.

Ryan found me about an hour later and asked me if I was all right. I wanted to make him happy. To make *myself* happy and say it was the best birthday party ever, but the truth was, it was not. It was probably the worst because I'd been unable to take part in any of it in any meaningful way and it made me feel bitchy. Even my conversation with the noted psychiatrist — I'd forgotten to ask him why he was noted — had been frustrating. But it had intrigued me and made me think.

Ryan drove me back to the hospital in silence and I gave him a hug and climbed out of the car. I knew he was watching me as I walked up to the entrance, so I tried to make my stride strong and confident, which wasn't difficult because I was feeling so frustrated and irritated at myself and everyone else.

chapter twenty-three

When I reached my room it occurred to me that I had to worry about Lucy and Kit murdering me in my sleep because I knew their secret. I was sitting alone on my bed and I was having that unnerving thought when Ella breezed in.

"Dr. Osborn has asked that you not leave the hospital until he sees you again."

"Why would he ask that?" I said.

"I'm sorry, but I'm afraid I don't know what he's thinking."

"But you're lovers, so you have a good chance of knowing." I watched her closely to see her reaction to my bald statement.

She was on her way out of the room, but she stopped and looked back at me, her face at first shocked and then angry and then both.

"Is that what Mavis found out?" I asked. "That you were lovers?"

"And why would that make the least bit of difference to anyone?"

"I doubt that Osborn's wife would like it. She has good reason to get rid of Mavis."

"Osborn's wife left him nine months ago!" she snapped, then spun on her heel and left the room.

Jesus, I thought. What did *that* mean? I paced the floor for a while, my thoughts wild in my head, and then I remembered the photocopies I had of Osborn's research papers and the "noted" psychiatrist's mention of a miracle memory pill. I read all four papers and then sat on my bed gazing out of the window. I wondered if the squirrel would appear. There was a fly caught between the two panes of glass trying desperately to find a way out, seeing freedom but being denied it by every bash of its body against the window. Sort of like me.

"What's up?" A familiar voice. I looked around as Martha came and sat down beside me on my bed. Her voice sounded thin and weak, but when I looked at her eyes they were clear and sharp. No fog. How many times had I been told that my eyes told the world whether or not I was well? When I was sick they weren't clear, they weren't bright, they were just dead.

I told her I'd been reading Osborn's research papers. "He did a small study with a new drug on rats and memory loss, and it looked promising for Alzheimer's patients."

"But?"

"There are no follow-up studies. All the research seems to have dried up for some reason"

I repeated what Brent Sebastien had said about Osborn's research being shut down. "I have a theory that makes Osborn my number-one suspect, but I need access to his computer to get answers."

"Answers to what?" asked Martha.

"To Mavis. To the relationship, if any, of his research to Mavis. To motive. To whether he killed her."

"You think he was ridding society of the weak and the sick?"

That dreadful thought hadn't occurred to me. "I don't know," I said. "His stalled research is a new lead. Maybe he didn't stop his research. Maybe he's still conducting it on the sly somehow."

"You mean he's experimenting on people and the drug may be killing them?"

"Don't know. That's why I need to get into his computer," I said. "Have you got your key-chain flash drive with you?"

Martha looked incredulous but nodded and went to get it from under her mattress — keys were definitely taboo in our rooms. As she took it off her key ring and gave it to me she said, "And just how are you going to access it?"

I just looked at her and smiled.

I lay in wait in the hall for Ella to appear and when she did I asked her if I could see Dr. Osborn, that it was urgent. She disappeared and I lounged against the wall outside the meds room. I could see Martha doing the same thing just down the hall. Ten minutes later Ella came back and said Dr. Osborn could see me. I followed her and she let me in through the door from the cafeteria, and then went back to the nursing station, knowing I knew the way.

I waited for two minutes and then opened the door to let Martha in. She placed the wooden wedge under the door to keep it ajar, in case anyone asked how she gained access. She went into the ladies' washroom while I went and knocked on Osborn's door. When I entered he got up and waved his hand to indicate that I should sit on the chair across from his desk. I'd never done that before and I guess my confusion showed.

"I have to go for dinner soon," he said, "so I can't take long with you."

I was about to reply when we both heard somebody crying. It was unmistakable, the kind of crying that comes from the heart, from the very soul of a person in agony.

With a glance at me, Dr. Osborn said, "Wait here, please," and he left the room.

I turned his laptop computer to face me and looked at his desktop. It was the cleanest desktop I'd ever seen. There were just four folders, all in Word or Excel, which I had on my computer: Research, Patients, Finances, and Hospital. I plugged my flash drive in and dragged the Research file over. But the patient files were too big. I looked through the directory of names and copied mine, Mavis's, and Minnie's, the patient with Alzheimer's who'd died in hospital. Martha was still sobbing in the hall as I pulled out the flash drive, returned the computer to its spot, and sat down again. I was looking at his family portrait when he came back in.

"I'm terribly sorry, Cordi. So, what was on your mind?" He sat down behind his desk. I was impressed. He was on a time constraint and he hadn't tried to shoo me out or use what had happened in the hall as an excuse to cut our meeting short.

So I said, "Too much," and should have known better. He was a psychiatrist, after all.

"Your mind's racing?"

I nodded. Didn't hurt to humour him, and besides, my mind *was* racing.

"We've just changed your meds. I don't want to try something else until we've given this a chance. You have to be patient."

"So why don't you want me to leave the hospital?"

"I just want to keep an eye on you with the new medication. But it's okay for you to go home tomorrow with your brother for a couple of hours."

Had Ryan invited me somewhere? I wondered. If he had I couldn't remember. Or had Osborn and Ryan been talking behind my back again? I didn't call the doctor on it and we talked about my meds for a while and then he gently disengaged by getting up and walking me to the door.

I went looking for Martha and found her in bed.

"You owe me one," she said thickly. "They jabbed me with a sedative and I've probably set back my discharge date by days."

"You can leave any time you want. You weren't committed." And then, more sympathetically, "You sounded so desperately unhappy! How the hell did you turn on the tears?"

"I recite the alphabet and think of all the sad things that have ever happened to me. I was crying by *M*."

How could Martha know that many sad things? She, who was always so happy?

Martha was really groggy, so I let her be and went to the nursing station to retrieve my computer. All our valuables were kept there, as well as power cords and anything we could use to harm ourselves. Spotty, though, because Martha hung on to her keys and keys could cause a lot of damage. But there was no one at the station, so I went back and got some money to buy a sandwich at the downstairs hospital cafeteria, which technically wasn't outside the hospital, so I figured it was all right.

As I was getting on the elevator Austin got on with me and we travelled down in our little box to somewhere between the second and the third floor, when it stopped. We were stuck and I used the intercom to find out what was wrong. A voice on the other end assured me that they were working on it. Austin and I stood in almost total silence for five minutes. He was congested and every time he breathed in, there was a little squeaky noise.

"It was for my father," he said out of the blue.

"What was?"

"The marijuana you saw me buy. It was for my father."

I didn't say anything.

"He's dying of cancer. There's a lot of pain. It helps."

Shit. I felt like a jerk and tried to apologize, but it sounded hollow even to me. But then again, maybe he was lying.

"You know what Mavis said to me the day before she supposedly died?" he said, changing the subject.

I waited.

"That she caught Ella stealing drugs from the medication room."

I rolled my eyes at the ceiling. Yet another motive for Ella. Which was more likely — that she gave Mavis the wrong medication and it killed her, or that she was stealing drugs for her own purposes? *Why not both?* I thought, feeling light-headed and frustrated. But in that moment I was suddenly pretty sure who'd killed Mavis. I just needed the *why* to tie it all up.

The elevator finally jerked to life and spat us out in the lobby, where we went our separate ways. I got a BLT and a chocolate milkshake and went to eat at the long counter by the windows. I wasn't keen on getting stuck in the elevator again, so I walked up the stairs.

By the time I opened the door to the seventh-floor lobby I was thoroughly winded, and the last thing I expected to see was Martha and my brother deep in conversation. She didn't look any the worse for wear and I marvelled at how fast the drug used to calm her had got out of her system. I wondered why the nurses had let her see Ryan at all.

I heard Ryan say, "Stop encouraging her," or something like that. I wasn't sure and it didn't make any sense. *What were they really saying?* I wondered. Ryan looked up and saw me and he put a hand on Martha's sleeve. She stopped talking and then they both smiled. The smiles looked forced, as though their mouths were stiff from too much talking.

Ryan gave me a hug.

"How's it going, Cordi?" he said lightly.

"Okay," I said. "Now you've got both of us in here. Whatever did you do to deserve that?"

His laughter, when it came, was overloud. "I just came to see how you and Martha were doing," he said.

"Does he know you're just acting?" I said to Martha.

She glanced at Ryan. "How else could I explain my being in here?"

Ryan was quiet and I wondered what he was thinking. I had a pretty good idea.

He perked up again and said, "We're having a small dinner party tomorrow night and wanted you both to come. I'll come and pick you up at six. I've cleared it with Dr. Osborn."

He gave me a quick hug and waved at Martha and then disappeared down the stairs I'd come up, leaving me feeling apprehensive and angry.

chapter twenty-four

When I pushed through the glass door to the seventh-floor common room, Martha was with me.

"When did Ryan clear it with Osborn and why did he feel he had to?" I asked her.

"I don't know," she replied.

I was not happy to hear that Ryan and Osborn had been talking about me again. The last time that had happened I'd ended up getting an ECT.

Martha let out a little whoop and I turned to see what had caused it. A big four-legged blond furball, a.k.a. a golden retriever, was sitting in the middle of the common room being mauled by Bradley and enjoying every minute. Bradley reminded me of someone, vaguely, as he buried his face in the dog's fur.

Lucy and Kit were hovering nearby and even Leo was there, keeping his distance, but watching intently. Austin was there, too, reading a book, pretending not to notice, but I saw him stealing a glance at the dog every now and then. Even Ella was there and smiling. It was a nice little vignette, all soft and warm and cuddly, just like the dog. It was amazing to watch the effect that the animal had on people. Everybody seemed relaxed and eager to befriend the beautifully groomed retriever with the long golden coat, lush-feathered tail, curly chest fur, and long silky floppy ears. The dog's handler was letting everyone have one-on-one time, and when it was Martha's turn, she asked, "What's its name?"

"Minnie," said the handler.

I saw Ella jerk like a puppet and struggle to keep the smile on her face. Minnie, the name of the Alzheimer's patient. *Interesting*, I thought. What did Ella know about Minnie?

Martha hogged the dog's time and I found myself becoming awfully impatient. I wanted to thrust Martha aside and have the dog all to myself. And I told her as much.

She let go of Minnie and I knelt down and hugged the dog as if my life depended on her accepting me. When I pulled back, she licked my face and I laughed and the sun broke through a cloud. A dog and a woman, caught in time.

I happened to look up and notice Jacques walking through the doorway of the common room. He stopped abruptly, then glanced at the handler with an odd expression on his face, or maybe I just imagined it, because it was so fleeting and was replaced by a smile at the scene before him. So odd to see so many smiles on a psychiatric ward. I was glad we were not considered dangerous because they would never have allowed the dog otherwise. But then again, someone *was* dangerous. And I was pretty sure that someone was Dr. Osborn.

I left Minnie and her admirers, collected my computer, and went back to my room, where I booted up the flash drive. And what I found there in Osborn's files made me shiver. So I lay down on my bed to think about it and fell asleep.

Something caught my attention. I sat up in bed and saw Kit standing by the door, immobile. I watched her as she opened the door and walked out, but this time she didn't open and close it nine times. She seemed strangely vacant and I got out of bed and opened the door to watch her walk down the hall, stepping on the lines without even noticing them. Something was wrong. I caught up to her and looked at her face. Her eyes were unblinking and I realized that she was sleepwalking. I knew enough to not try to wake her, at least that is what I had been taught. I stayed with her to make sure she didn't hurt herself. We passed by the nursing station but there was nobody there. I followed her into the cafeteria, hoping she would lie down on the sofa, but the door to the offices was ajar and she went through it, with me behind her. The corridor was dimly lit and as I walked toward Osborn's office, I felt suddenly disoriented, because Kit had disappeared.

I wasn't sure what to do when something was done to me. An arm snaked around my neck from behind and a hand clamped some tape over my mouth. I was pinned to the chest of my assailant and I struggled to get free. But I felt so weak, so strangely weak, and I knew I was in deep trouble. That awful sinking feeling you get when you know you are going down.

"It's okay, Cordi. This won't take long." I knew the voice, sickly, soothing. Osborn.

He was strong and he frogmarched me into the room where I had seen Mavis's running shoes under the bed so long ago. He wrestled me onto a metal bed and into some arm restraints and then had difficulty fastening the leg restraints because I was kicking like crazy. But he won and I lay there looking at him. He seemed so ordinary to be a killer. He started attaching electrodes to my head and I struggled to scream against the tape over my mouth. This couldn't be happening to me! I thought as my fear blossomed into full-blown terror.

He approached me with a shiny green pill in one hand and a scalpel in the other. "You have to swallow this pill, Cordi, before I paralyze you for the ECT."

I felt woozy from hyperventilating and desperate to keep the pill out of my mouth. The killer pill. If he got it into my mouth the tape would prevent me from spitting it out and it would slowly dissolve, while he waited patiently to zap me with electricity.

He peeled back part of the tape and I screamed. But he was fast and he was smart. As I screamed he shoved the pill into my open mouth and replaced the tape just as the door crashed open and Jacques came charging in. He caught Osborn off guard, butting his head into Osborn's stomach and taking him down. The pair were out of my line of sight now, but I could hear Jacques's fists making contact with Osborn's body, sickening thuds that seemed to go on and on.

Finally Jacques was standing over me, smiling. He whipped the tape off my mouth and I spat out the pill. It rolled onto the floor behind Jacques and he turned and stooped to pick it up. He walked close to me, holding the pill up to the light, and then he reached over, cupped my jaw in his hand, and stuffed the pill down my throat.

I sat up in bed so suddenly that I almost got whiplash. I felt my face for the tape but it wasn't there. It had been so *real!* Now I clung to my present reality, incredibly thankful that it had been a dream. But I lay trembling in bed as I remembered what I'd read on Osborn's files and realized I had a right to be afraid. I desperately needed to talk to Jacques or Martha.

I went in search of them. As luck would have it, I found them both in the cafeteria, sitting across from each other at a table. I wondered if they, too, had been talking about me.

"Who's the dog handler?" I asked bluntly. Everyone else had long gone, the dog was just a memory, and we were alone.

"What do you mean?" asked Jacques.

"You knew her. I saw the look on your face when you first saw her."

"Just an old friend," he said.

"Then why didn't you go up and say hello?"

"Cordi, don't be so rude," said Martha.

I was feeling quite paranoid, but for all I knew Minnie was an old police dog that Jacques had worked with and that was why he'd had a weird expression on his face. Then again, I'd never met a golden retriever that would make a good police dog. At first glimpse of a criminal Minnie would attack with tail wagging and tongue-slurping kisses. In answer to my question, Jacques just shrugged.

But I forgot about Minnie in my haste to tell them about Osborn. "It looks like he's our man," I said, relishing what was to come. They both looked over at me.

"How so?" said Jacques.

"He and his partner, David Ellison, were experimenting with rats using a new drug called Ecteril. It was supposed to help in memory loss for Alzheimer's patients."

I had their undivided attention. "At first the results were terrific and they published a paper saying as much."

"But something went wrong," said Jacques.

"Yes. Some of the rats began to die from strokes."

"How do you know this?" asked Jacques. Martha told him about my accessing Osborn's computer. Jacques looked stunned at our audacity.

"His trial records were all there on his desktop," I said.

"So rats were dying," said Jacques, recovering.

"And?" asked Martha.

"He had applied to start a clinical trial with human subjects on the basis of the results of the rat study," I said.

"Let me guess," said Jacques. "He was denied."

"That's right. They said no, the drug was too dangerous, end of story. Except I don't think it *was* the end of the story."

"Okay," said Jacques. "Shoot."

"I think they tried Ecteril on Ellison's old and dying Alzheimer's patients."

"What makes you think that?" asked Martha.

"There was a file on his desk a few days ago that I downloaded from his computer. A Minnie Anderson." I was watching Jacques closely. "She was an Alzheimer's patient under his partner's care."

"So what did you learn from it?" asked Martha.

"She was receiving a cocktail of drugs for various ailments: Aricept, Lipitor, Naprosyn, Ecteril, oxybutynin, and clonazepam."

I waited. Jacques was being infuriatingly silent. I knew he had spotted it, but it was Martha, who said, "Ecteril?"

"Exactly. Right, Jacques?" I said.

He looked at me and I could see sweat on his brow, but confusion in his eyes.

"You really are an undercover cop, aren't you, just as we said?" I asked.

He was silent, as if searching for something to say.

"What makes you think I'm a cop?" he finally said.

"I saw how you looked at Minnie's handler," I said impatiently.

"Minnie?" he asked. Man, he was good.

"The dog," I said.

"Right. The dog." When I said nothing he finally asked, "What about the dog?"

"She must belong to the daughter or relative or friend of your client, doesn't she?" I was winging it, hoping to catch him off guard.

"Come again?" Jacques cocked his head.

"Your client is Minnie Anderson's daughter, or at least some close relative," I said. "She's the dog handler, and she hired you to find out about her mother, Minnie. She obviously named the dog after her mother."

Jacques looked at me strangely.

"What made you go undercover?" I asked.

"Because there'd been a rash of unexplained deaths?" he said, almost as though he was just trying to please me. Very unnerving.

"And what does the dog have to do with all this?" he asked.

"Nothing, but you were hired to look into why Minnie died."

"Minnie died?" asked Martha, looking confused.

"Minnie had a stroke, a known side effect of Ecteril, according to Osborn's records," I said.

"And you think Osborn gave the drug to Minnie after his trials were aborted?" said Martha.

"Yes."

"But what does all this have to do with Mavis?" asked Jacques.

My theory was coming together just fine.

"I remember Mavis telling me about two little birds on a telephone wire when I first came here," I said.

"So?" asked Martha.

"She had completely forgotten the joke when I finally came back to the land of the living."

"So?" asked Martha again.

"So, suppose she had an ECT and was one of the unlucky ones to lose her memory," I said.

"Why is that important?" asked Martha.

"What if Osborn wasn't just working with Alzheimer's patients. What if he was looking into seeing if it would work on ECT patients, too?" I suggested.

"Would a drug designed for Alzheimer's patients work for ECT patients?" asked Jacques.

I was on a roll and wasn't really listening to him. I continued, "Osborn would need to choose a patient whose memory had been wiped by ECT. He'd then give her Ecteril and test her memory again after she had her *next* ECT. If her memory is good, then he'd know the Ecteril works."

"Slow down, Cordi," said Martha. "You're speaking too fast."

"After the last of Mavis's ECT treatments," I said, enunciating every syllable, "and just before she died, she remembered her stained T-shirt. The Ecteril worked! She didn't lose her memory that last time."

Bradley's quote from Hemingway rang through my head: *"It was a brilliant cure, but we lost the patient."*

"And Mavis," said Jacques, "was his guinea pig."

"Yes, but I think you already knew that," I said. "You were way too interested in my ECT when I told you I'd had one. You weren't interested in *me*. You were interested in what I knew or what I might find out. You even had lock picks and it was you who suggested there was a cover-up. You went so far as to almost get an ECT yourself so you could get some Ecteril and flush Osborn out, but you chickened out. Rightly so, it would seem. But you used me to track down Mavis's and Minnie's killer."

Jacques let out a whistle.

"And Osborn is after me now. I'm his next guinea pig."

And then an awful thought occurred to me. Maybe he had already given me Ecteril. Maybe he had given me more than one ECT and I had just assumed when he said 'another' that it meant a second one. I'd remembered Mavis's joke hadn't I? Or did she tell that to me before the first ECT and for some reason I had remembered the joke and little else? My mind was whirling with possibilities, but I wasn't dead so I hadn't taken the Ecteril. And if I had, I'd survived hadn't I?

chapter twenty-five

I left Martha and Jacques and went back to get my computer to look through Osborn's files again, specifically Mavis's. What I found there gave me the ammunition to go and see Osborn and have it out with him. I'd have to wait for morning, though, because the nurse told me he'd gone for the day. I was just packing up my computer to take it back to the nursing station when Ella walked in.

"Just wanted to know how you're doing," she said.

"Fine," I said.

"You don't have anything you want to talk about?"

I wondered what she was getting at. "Come to think of it," I said, "I *am* curious as to why you stopped trying to kill me."

She blinked, but showed no other signs of guilt.

"I saw you in Dr. Osborn's office," I told her. "You were crying."

Her face remained impassive.

"He broke up with you, didn't he? Osborn broke up with you and that's why you stopped trying to kill me. You didn't have to protect him anymore." Ella pulled on her ear, as if it were a lifeline.

"You knew about the Ecteril. You knew about Minnie. I saw how you reacted when you learned the dog's name."

She just stood there, quietly watching me.

"Or maybe it really is you, and not Osborn, who killed Mavis. She saw you stealing drugs from the medication room." I didn't really believe what I was saying but I wanted to see her reaction.

"Cordi, you know the medication room is just a distribution centre," said Ella "Only the drugs to be used on that day are there and they're individually wrapped for each patient. There is nothing to steal."

"Not even Ecteril?"

She didn't miss a beat.

"I don't know what you're talking about, Cordi. You need to try and rest your mind, clear everything out of it, and let the medication work."

She spent another fifteen minutes or so with me, trying to get me to talk about how I was feeling. But I was afraid I was going to bite her head off, so I said nothing until she made a move to leave.

"I need to talk to Dr. Osborn, please."

And finally her face registered something. But relief was not what I expected.

We'd arranged for me to see Osborn the next morning at 11:00 and I spent the hours before obsessing about what

I would say to him. I tried to marshal all my thoughts and arguments and accusations, worried that I would not be able to get it all together when I confronted Osborn. The thoughts were coming so fast and furious that I could see the faces of each of the people who might have killed Mavis, all of their motives, all of the minutiae of their lives, all like one vast wild chaotic kaleidoscope whirling out of control. But it all came down to Osborn. Of that I was sure.

I made a conscious effort to slow my mind and was trying to meditate when Ella came and got me. She let me through the door from the cafeteria without saying a word and I made my way down the hall to Osborn's door. I knocked and heard him call out to come in. I opened the door, and as I walked in he got up from his desk and walked around to greet me, his face haggard-looking, as if he knew what was coming.

"I know you killed Mavis," I said.

He motioned me to sit down. I sat in my usual spot and he sat across from me, as if I hadn't said anything. He pursed his lips and said, "Cordi, think it through. Why would I kill Mavis?"

"She killed your first wife?" I didn't really believe that, but I wanted to catch him off guard. And I did.

He looked absolutely flabbergasted. I went in for the kill.

"It was for the money then, wasn't it? You stood to make a fortune as the man who found the drug that would cure memory loss, not only in Alzheimer's patients but in ECT patients, too."

"It would be very exciting to discover such a drug."

"But you almost did. Ecteril."

He looked surprised.

"I read your and Ellison's study with rats and Ecteril."

"Then you must know some rats died and we pulled the plug on any future research. We weren't sure why or how it worked when it did, but it was too dangerous to pursue."

"Except you *did* pursue it. You couldn't resist the lure of fame and fortune and you tried it out on Minnie Anderson first, and you killed her."

"Minnie Anderson was old and died of natural causes."

"You cherry-picked your patients. You moved on from Alzheimer's patients to ECT patients. You earmarked those who'd had an ECT and suffered from memory loss, like Mavis. And then you gave them Ecteril to see if it worked to stop their short-term memory loss on the next ECT."

Osborn stared at me. It was disconcerting, but I continued, "That's why you were so interested to learn that Mavis had actually remembered spilling the juice on her shirt, a very short-term memory indeed. You knew it had worked." I paused for effect.

"You gave Mavis Ecteril and she died of a stroke because of it. How many others have died that we don't know about? How many more Alzheimer's patients did you kill before you moved on to us? And was I next on your list? Is that why you were so persistent about getting me to think about having another ECT? You knew I'd lost my memory. That made me the perfect candidate for Ecteril. Or have you already given me Ecteril?"

Osborn leaned forward in his chair and our eyes locked. "Listen, Cordi, do you remember my telling you about having the wrong premise, but everything you do based on that premise makes sense? Your delusions are based on the wrong premise — that Mavis died."

It sounded like a non sequitur to me. And besides, Mavis *did* die. I just couldn't seem to get this through to him.

He was about to say something else when the phone rang. *It always seemed to be ringing and interrupting us*, I thought angrily.

While he was on the phone and my thoughts were in turmoil, I looked around for something to calm myself. He had a bunch of magazines on the coffee table, but there was also a plastic stand-up picture frame with some words on it that either hadn't been there before or that I hadn't noticed. I reached over and picked it up.

My desolate mind cannot erase
The darkness within … it's God's disgrace

So the poem had spoken to Dr. Osborn, too.

"Chilling in its accuracy, isn't it?" said Osborn, hanging up the phone.

"'God's disgrace' — it's very haunting," I agreed.

"My son wrote it," said Osborn with more than a touch of parental pride.

And suddenly everything came together for me.

chapter twenty-six

"So Bradley's your son?" I couldn't resist looking at his family portrait, at a young Bradley. That was who Bradley had reminded me of earlier — of his younger self, the boy still evident in the man.

Osburn looked at me thoughtfully, before replying, "That's confidential, if you don't mind. He doesn't want people to think he's getting preferential treatment."

But I'd seen them together at the hockey game. Anyone else could have, too, and think he was getting preferential treatment.

"And is he?" I said.

Osborn pursed his lips, but said nothing.

"Was he why you were pushing your experiments with Ecteril? To help your son?"

I paused, then went on, "He was terrified of ECT, afraid he'd lose his memory like Hemingway, but what if everything else had failed? That all that was left to try was ECT? What wouldn't a parent do to ease the fear?"

"Listen to yourself, Cordi. It's all in your head. The research was discontinued because it was too dangerous."

"But your son kept pushing you, didn't he? That's who you were talking to on the phone when you said, 'It's been stopped. It's out of my hands.'"

He stared at me from across his desk.

"But it wasn't out of your son's hands, was it? And you knew the minute I told you that Mavis remembered the juice being spilled on her T-shirt."

It was all coming clear to me, like fog consumed by the sun, leaving nothing but clarity.

"And Bradley was desperate. Suppose he stole some Ecteril from you and tried it out on Mavis first, just to make sure it was okay, in his deluded reasoning."

I saw Osborn start at that and I knew I'd hit a nerve.

I was suddenly anxious to get out of there, afraid Osborn would put me in a straitjacket and ship me off somewhere to silence me. I ran from his office, then down the hall and through the door to the cafeteria and into the common room. I literally bumped into Austin as he came through the door from the lobby.

We untangled ourselves and I looked him in the eye and said, "Was Bradley going to give you a pill that would stop the memory loss of ECT?'

Austin gave me an odd look and started to move away from me.

"I don't know what you're talking about," he said. But I knew he did.

"Don't take it," I called after him. "It'll kill you."

Ella came up to me then and I turned to her and said, "But you're not trying to kill me anymore, are you? I know why now. It wasn't Osborn, it was his son. You stopped

Suzanne F. Kingsmill

when you found out that Dr. Osborn's son had killed Mavis by using her as a guinea pig — giving her Ecteril — before taking it himself. Or maybe he didn't even know about Minnie's death and gave the pill to Mavis because, like him, she was so desperately afraid of losing her memory."

Ella reached out her hand as if to take me by the shoulder, but I backed away.

"It wasn't Dr. Osborn," I continued. "You must have been very relieved. But didn't it bother you that there had been others? I overheard you saying that, that there had been others."

She sighed and said in a voice that reeked of patience, "If you overheard me saying something about others, it would have been about all the other suicide victims I've seen in my career."

She seemed so calm and believable that it confused me and made me feel very uneasy.

"Cordi, I think you should go back to your room and lie down for a while. You need to calm down."

I did need calming down, that was for sure, but I also wanted to talk to Bradley. To throw Ella off, I headed down the hallway toward my room and met Jacques coming in the opposite direction.

"What's up?" he asked. "You look terrible."

"You have to arrest Osborn," I said. "He did it. And while you're at it arrest his father, too. They're both guilty."

"What are you talking about?" said Jacques as he grabbed me by the arms.

"Bradley," I said. "He's Osborn's son."

Jacques looked taken aback.

"Don't you see? It was Bradley who killed Mavis. He knew about his father's research. He knew Ecteril worked for memory loss. He must have been frantic when the research was halted. They both must have been. Father wanting the son to get better. The son desperate to get better."

"So he stole some from his father?" asked Jacques.

"He was afraid to have ECT, even though it stood a good chance of helping him. He was a writer. Like Hemingway he was afraid he'd lose his memory."

"So why not just take the drug? Why give it to Mavis?" We'd been over this territory before.

"He must have known it had killed at least one person. He needed to know if it was safe and not just an aberration. So he weaseled his way into her good books by pretending to be a Scientologist and convinced her to take the pill."

"How would he have known that it was a potential killer?" asked Jacques.

"Maybe his father told him, to explain why he was stopping the research."

"So he used Mavis."

"Bradley told me he was terrified of ECT and I saw him give something to Mavis just before she had another ECT. I'm sure it was Ecteril and she took it after she spilled her juice. I saw her put her hand to her mouth."

"How do you know it's not the father?"

"Because he was genuinely surprised when I told him Mavis had remembered her juice-stained T-shirt. He knew ECT affected her memory and when this particular treatment didn't, he must have asked why. That's when he must have known she'd received Ecteril, and the only one who could have given it to her, besides himself, was his son. He must have been horrified."

"What if Bradley didn't know Ecteril was a killer?"

I was getting impatient. Jacques was asking too many questions, instead of doing something. He was a cop, after all. I ignored him and said, "Bradley was scheming to use Austin as his next guinea pig." And I told Jacques what Martha had overheard in the men's washroom. It jibed with what Bradley had said about trying again.

"And you have to arrest them," I said.

"Why me?"

Did he really have to ask that question? "Because I know you are law enforcement of some kind."

He'd relaxed his grip on my arms but he hadn't let go, and suddenly he pulled me to him in a big hug and whispered in my ear, "But on what grounds, Cordi? We have no proof."

I tried to pull away from him, but he held me tightly, and then our lips touched in a gentle kiss that suddenly got legs. But I had work still to do. Surely he saw that? I was too excited about solving the case to do anything but squirm out of his arms.

"I have Osborn's files that reveal he put Minnie on Ecteril," I said. "That will give you grounds. I'll go and get the flashdrive and give it to you. Then you'll see."

He tried to hold me back, but I was on a mission.

"It was always you, and only you, that I was interested in," he whispered as he let me go.

He looked sad, but I had no time to deal with that right now. I brushed past him to my room before he could say anything more. No one was there. I went to my bedside table and pulled out the drawer to get the flashdrive. But the drawer was empty. I looked everywhere, but there was no flashdrive. Had I left it somewhere? I was trying to straighten out all the thoughts in my head when Ella came in to tell me Ryan was here to pick me up. It seemed too early for Ryan but I got my coat and put on my boots and walked down the hall.

Jacques materialized by my side and said, "Are you okay?"

"Did you take care of the Osborns?"

"Not to worry," he said. "Everything's just fine."

But he didn't look as though everything was fine. He looked worried, as though there was something wrong with me. And the sadness was still there. *Why is he sad?* I wondered.

I could see Ryan waiting in the seventh-floor lobby and I was itching to tell him everything. Jacques walked me to the elevators and Ryan gave me a hug. Then we stood and waited for the elevator. "Where's Martha?" I asked.

"She's coming," Ryan said, and then the elevator doors opened and I forgot about Martha as my world shattered before me.

As I stared at the woman stepping out of the elevator I was presented with two equally unappetizing and repugnant possibilities. One: some or everything that had happened before the elevator door opened had been a delusion; or two: I was hallucinating right now.

Either way I was in trouble, because the woman on the elevator was Mavis.

chapter twenty-seven

I stood transfixed as she smiled at me and walked on by as if nothing had happened. There were cries of "Mavis, you're back!" and people gathered around her. I was aware of Ryan standing there open-mouthed, watching Kit give Mavis a hug. He turned to look at me and what he saw galvanized him into action. He took me by the arm and led me into the elevator. When I turned and before the doors closed, I saw Jacques looking at me, his face contorted in surprise. I could feel my own face expressing the shock I felt and I tried to hide it, but judging by the look on Jacques's face, mine was worse than I thought. And then the elevator doors shut and I felt like I was being spirited away at the denouement of a book.

We sat in Ryan's car in the parking lot for twenty minutes waiting for Martha, and Ryan kept looking at me, trying to read my mood, I guess. We hardly spoke until Martha finally arrived and got in the back seat. Ryan wheeled the car out onto the street and headed west.

"So she's alive," he said.

"Who's alive?" said Martha.

"Mavis," said Ryan.

"But I thought she was dead," said Martha.

There was a painful silence.

"Mavis never died," said Ryan.

"Am I delusional?" I asked.

There was a godawful long silence before Ryan said, "Sometimes."

"If I was delusional, why did you go along with me?" I asked.

"I didn't," said Ryan.

"I meant Martha," I said. I turned to look at her.

Her smile was sickly as she said, "Because I believed you." She gave a half laugh. "You always said I was gullible. But you made perfect sense, as long as Mavis was dead."

Perfect sense. I thought back to what Austin and Osborn had said about things being logical, as long as the premise was right. Dear God, had I really got the premise wrong, or was *this* moment in time the wrong one, and my days in hospital the right ones?

The evening was the longest one of my life, because Ryan's wife had invited some friends over and I had to try to make small talk. Ryan wanted me to stay the night — he said he'd persuaded Dr. Osborn to let me stay the night — but when I learned that, I was adamant about going home for a while. The fact that nothing was as it seemed, was tormenting me. My heart lurched when I thought of Jacques. Was my relationship with him a delusion, too, or was it real? Martha dropped me off and tried to invite herself in, but I just wanted to be alone. I watched her tail lights as she drove out of the circular driveway and onto Douglas Crescent. I turned away then and walked into the alcove that I share with my neighbours, and there he was, sitting on my doorstep, Jacques.

He stood up as I came through the archway. We stood there eyeing each other like two friends after a fight, except we hadn't had a fight. We'd just had the total implosion of my mind, if I could believe what I'd seen at the hospital and what my brother had said, and if I did, it meant that I didn't know if Jacques was really my lover or not. I felt vulnerable, scared, and unwanted. And then Jacques opened his arms and I melted right into them, like a hand to a glove.

We didn't speak and we didn't make it to my bedroom. We barely made it through the front door before his hands found the buttons on my shirt and the belt to my pants, his lips found my mouth, then his hand my breast, in a cascading journey of love and desire and sexual astonishment. And his strength was wildly exciting because, in that moment, I knew he would never hurt me. I was deliciously lost in the moment.

We were lying on my sofa in that surreal afterglow, my head on his shoulder, his arms encircling me. I could feel his chest rise and fall in a hypnotic rhythm that might have put me to sleep if I hadn't been thinking about Mavis.

"Why did you humour me?" My head rose and fell with his chest.

Finally he said, "You were believable. It was all highly plausible, if Mavis was dead."

Martha had said the same thing.

"And besides, why would you lie?" he said.

"Meaning?"

"You had nothing to gain by saying Mavis was dead when she wasn't. So she must have died. But I started to suspect something when you told me I was an undercover cop."

"You're not?" I said, trying hard to keep my mind from sliding out of control.

He squeezed me and said, "If I was an undercover cop, which I'm not, I'd have to be the worst one in history because I let you do all the work."

I realized then that he had never actually said he was or wasn't a cop.

"Why didn't you say you weren't a cop?" I asked.

"Pride. You seemed so excited that I was a cop."

"Why would you continue to help me solve the murder, then?" I asked, waiting to poke holes in his arguments.

"Because until I saw Mavis today, I wasn't sure that you were delusional. You seemed so normal. I thought I was helping you. I thought it was the right thing to do."

He kissed the top of my head and then in a whisper said, "And because I am falling in love with you."

I felt a sudden rushing sensation in my head and a prickling heat all over my body. He squeezed me again and I squeezed him back. I felt I should say something into the growing silence, but "I love you, too" sounded too much like an afterthought.

At last I said, "You believed me about the subway and the bridge."

"It was logical, based on the assumption that someone was trying to kill you. But nobody was."

"But I *was* pushed onto the subway tracks and over the bridge."

"They must have been dreams, Cordi, or particularly vivid hallucinations."

I thought back to the morning after my fall from the bridge. There had been no marks on me, even though there should have been, and the coat I had left behind, rolled up in a ball in the ravine, had been hanging in my closet the next morning. Had the police been a delusion, too?

"And the morgue?" I said.

"That was real. I wanted to know if you were right."

We lay in silence for a while until I said, "But I saw Bradley give something to Mavis just before she had an ECT. It was the Ecteril."

"It was a candy," said Jacques.

How many other candies had there been? I wondered.

"But you're not a delusion," I said.

"No, never was, never will be." We lapsed into silence.

After a few minutes he said, "We can get you more help, Cordi. We can beat this, whatever it is."

As I lay there with my head snuggled on Jacques's shoulder, I felt a sudden spasm of anger and all my misgivings suddenly evaporated. What had happened to me *had* been real. I was right. I knew I was right. It had all happened exactly as I remembered it. It wasn't Mavis I had seen on the elevator. It was someone who looked like Mavis because Bradley *had* given his father's pill to Mavis to see if it worked, and she *had* had a stroke and died. Ella *had* tried to cover it up, thinking that Dr. Osborn had killed Mavis. And then she *had* tried to kill me when it looked like I was going to expose Osborn. It was all so obvious, looked at from my point of view. Why didn't anybody else see it?

I was right.

And everybody else was wrong.

Weren't they?

acknowledgements

Thanks to my two sons, Tim and Jesse, for always being there for me and who read and critiqued an earlier draft of *Crazy Dead*. Thanks to my sister, Dorion, for having my back. To Sandy — just because. And thanks to K.G. and J.K. for helping me through some tough times, but times that made this book possible. And to my parents, who never gave up on me.

Thanks also to the team at Dundurn!

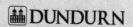

VISIT US AT

Dundurn.com
@dundurnpress
Facebook.com/dundurnpress
Pinterest.com/dundurnpress